Counterfeit Capitalist
Shane Reed

Copyright

Copyright © 2024 by Shane Reed

All rights reserved.

No portion of this book may be reproduced in any form without written permission from the publisher or author, except as permitted by U.S. copyright law.

Chapter 1

Tom Beauchamp squinted at the brake pad in his hand, turning it over as he inspected every curve and edge. The factory floor hummed with the usual cacophony of machinery, but Tom's keen ears picked up an out-of-place sound.

"Hey, Frank!" he called out, a smirk tugging at his lips. "You trying to sneak a nap in the supply closet again?"

A muffled thud followed by a string of curses answered him. Moments later, a disheveled Frank emerged, rubbing his elbow.

"How'd you know, boss?" Frank grumbled, his face flushed with embarrassment.

Tom chuckled, setting down the brake pad. "Your snoring could wake the dead, Frank. Maybe try the roof next time – might muffle the sound a bit."

As Frank shuffled back to his station, Tom shook his head, a fond smile on his face. Despite the stress of running the factory, moments like these reminded him why he enjoyed it. The camaraderie, the shared laughs – it made the long hours bearable.

His thoughts were interrupted by the click of heels on concrete. Tom's heart skipped a beat as he turned to see Giselle striding towards him, her red hair catching the afternoon sunlight streaming through the high windows.

"Giselle?" he said, surprised. "What brings you here?"

She approached with a mischievous glint in her green eyes. "Can't a girl surprise her hardworking boyfriend?"

Tom's mind raced. Was it their anniversary? Her birthday? He was sure he hadn't forgotten anything important.

Giselle laughed, reading his panic. "Relax, Tom. I was in the neighborhood and thought I'd stop by."

Relief washed over him, followed quickly by curiosity. "In the neighborhood? This industrial park isn't exactly on the way to anywhere."

She shrugged, her eyes darting around the factory floor. "Maybe I just wanted to see where all the magic happens."

Tom raised an eyebrow. There was something she wasn't telling him, but he knew better than to push. Giselle's curiosity often led her down interesting paths, and he'd learned to enjoy the ride.

"Well, you're just in time for the grand tour," he said, offering his arm with exaggerated gallantry. "Shall we begin with the riveting world of friction coefficients?"

Giselle rolled her eyes but took his arm, her touch sending a warm thrill through him. As they started walking, Tom couldn't help but wonder what had really brought her here today. Whatever it was, he had a feeling life was about to get a lot more interesting.

Tom guided Giselle through the maze of machinery, their footsteps echoing off the concrete floor. As they reached his cramped office, he gestured to a rickety chair.

"Not exactly the Ritz, is it?" he said with a self-deprecating chuckle.

Giselle perched on the edge of the seat, her eyes roaming the cluttered space. "It's... cozy," she offered diplomatically.

Tom leaned against his desk, studying her face. "So, what's the real reason for this surprise visit? Not that I'm complaining, mind you."

She hesitated, then said, "I was thinking... maybe we could do something special tonight? Get dressed up, go somewhere nice for dinner?"

Tom's heart sank. He knew that tone – it was the same one she'd used when suggesting they look at houses outside the city last month. "Giselle, you know I'd love to, but—"

"But you're swamped with work," she finished, a hint of resignation in her voice.

He nodded, guilt gnawing at him. "I'm sorry. Things are just so tight right now. Maybe next month?"

Giselle's smile didn't quite reach her eyes. "Of course. I understand."

Tom's gaze drifted to the newspaper on his desk, desperate for a distraction. A headline caught his eye: "Master Counterfeiter Caught After Decade-Long Spree."

"Can you believe this?" he said, picking up the paper. "Guy printed millions before they caught him."

Giselle leaned forward, her curiosity piqued. "Really? How'd he manage that?"

As Tom began explaining the intricacies of the counterfeiter's scheme, a spark ignited in his mind. The gears started turning, possibilities unfolding. For the first time in years, he felt a rush of excitement.

Maybe, just maybe, there was a way out of this endless grind after all.

Tom's eyes glazed over as he leaned back in his creaky office chair, the hum of machinery from the factory floor fading into the background. In his mind's eye, he saw himself strutting down a sun-drenched beach, a suitcase overflowing with crisp hundred-dollar bills in each hand.

"Mr. Beauchamp," a bikini-clad woman called out, "your private yacht is ready!"

He grinned, imagining himself tossing a handful of bills into the air. "Keep the change, sweetheart!"

A chuckle escaped his lips, drawing him back to reality. Tom shook his head, running a hand through his graying hair. "Get it together, old man," he muttered to himself.

The door creaked open, and Tom straightened up as Jerry, one of his long-time employees, poked his head in. "Boss? Got a minute?"

"For you, Jerry? Always," Tom replied, gesturing to the chair across from his desk. "What's on your mind?"

Jerry eased into the seat, his work-worn hands fidgeting with his cap. "It's about the new brake pad design. We've hit a snag in production."

Tom leaned forward, his brow furrowing. "Talk to me. What kind of snag?"

As Jerry explained the technical issues, Tom listened intently, occasionally jotting down notes. His eyes carried a familiar weariness, but his voice remained steady and focused.

"Alright," Tom said after Jerry finished, "let's head down to the floor and take a look. We'll figure this out together."

Standing up, Tom felt a twinge in his back – a reminder of the countless hours he'd spent hunched over this very desk. He stretched, trying to work out the kink, and thought to himself, "There's got to be more to life than this. But for now, the factory needs me."

With a deep breath, he followed Jerry out, ready to tackle yet another problem in a long line of challenges that seemed to have no end.

Tom reached for his coffee mug, his mind still churning with thoughts of production issues and design flaws. As he lifted the mug to his lips, his elbow caught the edge of a stack of papers, sending them cascading across his desk.

"Oh, for Pete's sake," he grumbled, instinctively jerking back. The sudden movement caused the hot coffee to slosh over the rim, creating a steaming brown stain down the front of his crisp white shirt.

"Gah!" Tom yelped, jumping to his feet. The mug slipped from his fingers, clattering onto the desk and spilling its remaining contents across his carefully organized documents. "Oh, come on! Really?"

Just then, Giselle breezed into the office, her green eyes widening at the scene before her. "Tom! What happened?"

Tom looked up, his face a mixture of frustration and embarrassment. "I'm starting to think this factory is conspiring against me," he said, attempting to dab at his shirt with a handful of tissues.

Giselle sprang into action, her petite frame moving with purpose. "Here, let me help," she said, her soft Quebecois accent tinged with concern. She grabbed a box of tissues from a nearby shelf and began mopping up the spilled coffee from the desk.

"Thanks, Giselle," Tom sighed, watching as she expertly salvaged the wet documents. "I don't know what I'd do without you."

Giselle flashed him a warm smile. "Probably drown in a sea of coffee and paperwork," she teased. She rummaged through a drawer and produced a small sewing kit. "Now, take off your shirt."

Tom raised an eyebrow. "Excuse me?"

"Your shirt, Tom," Giselle repeated, threading a needle. "I can't sew it while you're wearing it. Unless you want to explain to your employees why you're walking around shirtless."

Tom chuckled, unbuttoning his shirt. "You're a lifesaver, you know that?"

As Giselle worked on the coffee stain, Tom couldn't help but marvel at her resourcefulness. "Where did you learn to do all this?" he asked.

"Growing up in a small town, you learn to make do," she replied, her nimble fingers working quickly. "Besides, someone has to keep you presentable, Mr. Big-Shot Factory Owner."

Tom smiled, a warmth spreading through his chest that had nothing to do with the spilled coffee. In that moment, amid the chaos of his office, he felt a profound gratitude for Giselle's presence in his life.

Tom leaned against his desk, watching Giselle work her magic on his shirt. "You know, if we play our cards right, maybe one day you won't have to patch up my clothes anymore," he mused, a hint of playfulness in his voice.

Giselle looked up, her green eyes twinkling. "Oh? And what grand scheme are you cooking up in that head of yours, Tom Beauchamp?"

"I'm thinking... private island, crystal-clear waters, umbrella drinks," Tom said, gesturing dramatically with his hands. "You, me, and not a single brake pad in sight."

Giselle laughed, the sound light and melodic. "And how exactly do you plan on affording this island paradise? Last I checked, brake pads weren't exactly raking in the millions."

Tom winked at her. "I've got ideas, darling. Big ideas."

As Giselle finished her handiwork, Tom slipped his shirt back on and moved towards the large factory window. The late afternoon sun cast long shadows across the factory floor, where workers moved about their tasks with practiced efficiency. He pressed his palm against the cool glass, his eyes unfocusing as he gazed at the familiar scene.

"Sometimes," he said softly, almost to himself, "I wonder if this is all there is. Wake up, make brake pads, go home, repeat."

Giselle came up behind him, wrapping her arms around his waist. "Is that so bad?" she asked gently.

Tom sighed, his breath fogging the window. "It's not bad, it's just... predictable. Safe." He turned to face her, his eyes reflecting a mix of weariness and determination. "Don't you ever wonder what else is out there? What we could achieve if we just... took a chance?"

Tom took a deep breath, his eyes locked on Giselle's. "I've been thinking about something... something big," he said, his voice low and measured. "What if I told you I had a plan that could change everything for us?"

Giselle's eyebrows shot up, her green eyes widening with curiosity. "I'm listening," she said, a hint of caution in her tone.

Tom glanced around the factory floor, then leaned in close. "Counterfeiting," he whispered, the word hanging in the air between them.

Giselle's jaw dropped. "Tom!" she hissed, instinctively looking around to make sure no one had overheard. "Are you out of your mind?"

"Just hear me out," Tom said, holding up his hands. "I've done the research. With my attention to detail and your artistic skills, we could pull this off. We could finally have the life we've always dreamed of."

Giselle shook her head, her red hair swaying. "It's illegal, Tom. Not to mention dangerous. We could end up in prison!"

"Or we could end up on that private island," Tom countered, his eyes sparkling with excitement. "Think about it, Giselle. No more worrying about bills, no more endless days in this factory. We could be free."

Giselle bit her lip, her brow furrowed in thought. "I don't know, Tom. It's a huge risk."

Tom took her hands in his, his touch gentle but insistent. "Sometimes the biggest risks lead to the greatest rewards. We've always talked about taking a chance, making a change. This could be our opportunity."

Giselle looked into Tom's eyes, searching. She saw the weariness there, but also a fire she hadn't seen in years. Slowly, almost imperceptibly, she nodded.

"Alright," she said softly. "Let's do it. But promise me we'll be careful."

Tom's face broke into a wide grin. He pulled Giselle close, planting a kiss on her forehead. "We're in this together," he said. "You and me against the world."

As they stood there, wrapped in each other's arms, the factory hummed around them. The future stretched out before them, full of possibility and danger in equal measure. Whatever came next, they would face it side by side.

Chapter 2

The acrid smell of burning rubber assaulted Tom's nostrils as he stepped onto the factory floor. He winced, his temples throbbing from another restless night. The familiar cacophony of machinery drowned out his sigh as he surveyed the sea of employees, all busily crafting brake pads with mechanical precision.

"Morning, boss!" chirped Francois, a lanky teenager with an unfortunate mustache attempt. "Ready for another thrilling day in paradise?"

Tom forced a smile. "You know it, Francois. Nothing gets my motor running like the sweet symphony of industrial manufacturing."

As he made his way through the maze of conveyor belts, Tom's mind wandered to the vacation brochures stuffed in his desk drawer. Pristine beaches, luxurious resorts—a world away from the grime and monotony of his current existence.

"Heads up!" A voice snapped him back to reality just as a stray brake pad whizzed past his ear.

"Thanks, Giselle," Tom said, turning to face his girlfriend. Her fiery red hair was tied back in a messy bun, grease smudges adorning her freckled cheeks. "Your lightning-fast reflexes never cease to amaze me. You'd make a great getaway driver."

Giselle raised an eyebrow. "Planning a heist, are we? And here I thought we were just honest, hardworking folk."

Tom chuckled, but something in her words struck a chord. "Speaking of which," he said, lowering his voice, "I've got something to show you later. Meet me in the office after lunch?"

Curiosity flickered in Giselle's green eyes. "Ooh, mysterious. I do love a man with secrets."

As she sauntered away, Tom couldn't help but marvel at how she managed to make even a grimy factory uniform look alluring. He shook his head, refocusing on the task at hand.

The morning dragged on, each minute feeling like an eternity. Tom's mind kept drifting to the folded newspaper article hidden in his pocket. He'd read it so many times he could recite it from memory:
"Local Man Arrested in Million-Dollar Counterfeiting Scheme."
The words danced in his head, a siren song of possibility. He imagined himself lounging on a yacht, sipping champagne, far from the mundane grind of brake pad production. The risk was enormous, but so was the potential reward.

Finally, lunchtime arrived. Tom retreated to his office, pulling out the crumpled article. He spread it on his desk, studying the grainy photo of the handcuffed counterfeiter. The man's expression was a mix of defeat and... was that a hint of pride?

A soft knock interrupted his musings. Giselle poked her head in, her curious gaze immediately landing on the newspaper.

"So," she said, closing the door behind her, "what's this big secret you've been dying to share?"

Tom took a deep breath, his heart racing. This was it—the moment that could change everything. He gestured for Giselle to sit down, his mind scrambling for the right words.

"Giselle," he began, his voice barely above a whisper, "how would you feel about taking a little... detour from the straight and narrow?"

Tom's fingers flew across the keyboard, his eyes darting between multiple screens as he delved deeper into the intricate world of U.S. currency design. The soft glow of the monitor illuminated his face, highlighting the growing bags under his eyes and the stubble on his chin.

"Who knew there were so many secrets hidden in a dollar bill?" he muttered to himself, zooming in on a microscopic security feature.

Giselle's voice floated in from the kitchen. "Tom, it's 3 AM. Are you still at it?"

"Just a few more minutes," he called back, not taking his eyes off the screen. "Did you know there are exactly 13 arrows in the eagle's talons on the back of a dollar? Symbolism for the original 13 colonies."

He heard Giselle's footsteps approaching. She leaned over his shoulder, her presence a mix of concern and curiosity. "Fascinating. But maybe it's time for a break?"

Tom sighed, rubbing his eyes. "You're right. It's just... there's so much to learn. Every time I think I've got it figured out, I discover another layer of complexity."

Giselle squeezed his shoulder. "Rome wasn't built in a day, and neither will your... project."

Tom chuckled, closing his laptop. "True. But Rome didn't have to worry about color-shifting ink and watermarks."

The next morning, Tom found himself on the phone, adopting a fake British accent as he spoke to a paper mill representative in China.

"Yes, hello. This is Dr. Archibald Featherbottom from the Royal Institute of Currency Studies," he said, trying not to laugh at his own ridiculous pseudonym. "I'm conducting research on various types of paper used in global currencies. Might I inquire about your cotton-linen blend options?"

As he jotted down notes, Tom couldn't help but marvel at his own audacity. Here he was, a former brake pad manufacturer, now masquerading as a British academic to source paper for counterfeit money. Life had certainly taken an unexpected turn.

"Of course, we'd need samples," Tom continued, his faux accent slipping slightly. "For purely academic purposes, you understand."

As he hung up the phone, a mix of excitement and trepidation washed over him. He'd just taken another step down this dangerous path. But as he looked at the stacks of research surrounding him, he couldn't help but feel a thrill of anticipation. He was in too deep to turn back now.

Tom stood in the dimly lit warehouse, his eyes scanning the vast empty space. The musty smell of disuse filled his nostrils as he paced the concrete floor, his footsteps echoing in the cavernous room.

"This'll do nicely," he muttered to himself, running a hand through his graying hair. "Plenty of space, out of the way, and best of all, no questions asked."

He pulled out a small notebook and began jotting down measurements and notes. His mind raced with plans for the sophisticated printing setup he'd need to replicate the intricate designs of U.S. currency.

"Alright, let's see," Tom murmured, tapping his pen against his chin. "We'll need the offset press here, the intaglio press there, and a secure area for drying and cutting..."

As he meticulously plotted out each detail, a nagging voice in the back of his mind whispered doubts. Tom paused, his pen hovering over the paper.

"What am I doing?" he asked aloud, his voice barely above a whisper. "This isn't just bending the rules, it's... it's full-on criminal."

He closed his eyes, took a deep breath, and exhaled slowly. When he opened them again, his gaze fell on the worn leather briefcase containing his life savings.

"No," Tom said firmly, straightening his shoulders. "I've come too far to back out now. This is my chance for a better life, and I'm going to take it."

With renewed determination, he returned to his planning, carefully sketching out the layout for his counterfeit operation. As he worked, Tom couldn't help but marvel at the irony of his situation.

"Who would've thought," he chuckled softly, "that all those years of managing production lines would come in handy for this?"

Tom's heart raced as he surveyed the nondescript warehouse he'd rented on the outskirts of town. The hum of machinery filled the air, a symphony of possibility that sent shivers down his spine.

"This is it," he whispered, running his hand along the sleek surface of the intaglio press. "My ticket to the good life."

Visions of tropical beaches and luxury cars danced in his head as he imagined the stacks of crisp bills that would soon be rolling off these presses. The risk was enormous, but the potential payoff? Unimaginable.

A sharp knock on the door jolted Tom from his reverie. He tensed, then relaxed as he remembered his appointment. With a deep breath, he opened the door to reveal a tall, distinguished-looking man in an impeccably tailored suit.

"Mr. Beauchamp, I presume?" The man's voice was smooth as silk, with a hint of an accent Tom couldn't quite place.

"That's me," Tom replied, extending his hand. "And you must be Patrice Dubois."

Patrice's grip was firm, his piercing blue eyes seeming to look right through Tom. "Indeed. I must say, your operation here is... impressive."

Tom felt a surge of pride. "Well, I've always believed in doing things right."

Patrice chuckled, a sound that was both warm and slightly unnerving. "A commendable attitude. Though in our line of work, perhaps 'right' is a relative term, no?"

Tom shifted uncomfortably. "I suppose so. But I'm just trying to get ahead, you know? Make a better life for myself."

"Ah, the American Dream," Patrice mused, running a finger along the edge of the printing press. "Or should I say, the Canadian version? Tell me, my friend, have you considered the moral implications of your endeavor?"

Tom blinked, caught off guard. "I... well, I mean, I know it's not exactly legal, but-"

Patrice held up a hand, his eyes twinkling with amusement. "Please, spare me the justifications. In my experience, morality is often just a luxury for those who can afford it. And soon, my friend, you'll be able to afford quite a lot of it."

Tom's hands trembled as he carefully placed the engraved plate onto the printing press. He took a deep breath, hoping this attempt would finally yield results. With a determined nod, he pulled the lever.

The machine whirred to life, the familiar smell of ink filling the air. Tom watched intently as the paper fed through, his heart racing with anticipation. As the first bill emerged, his excitement quickly turned to dismay.

"Damn it!" he exclaimed, snatching up the freshly printed note. The image was blurry, the intricate details of the dollar bill lost in a smudged mess.

Giselle peered over his shoulder, her green eyes twinkling with amusement. "Well, mon chéri, I don't think even a blind cashier would accept that one."

Tom ran a hand through his graying hair, frustration etched on his face. "I don't understand. I've followed every step to the letter."

Giselle placed a comforting hand on his arm. "Perhaps it's time for a break? You've been at this for hours."

"I can't stop now," Tom insisted, already preparing for another attempt. "We're so close, I can feel it."

As he adjusted the plate, Tom's mind wandered to the potential payoff. All these sleepless nights and failed attempts would be worth it once they started producing flawless bills. He could almost taste the freedom that money would bring.

Giselle's voice cut through his reverie. "You know, I've been thinking. What if we tried adjusting the pressure on the press? It might help with the clarity issue."

Tom paused, considering her suggestion. "That... actually makes sense. How did you come up with that?"

She shrugged, a mischievous smile playing on her lips. "Let's just say I've been doing some light reading on printing techniques. Someone has to keep you from going completely mad in this endeavor."

Tom couldn't help but chuckle. "What would I do without you, Giselle?"

"Probably print money that looks like it went through the wash," she quipped, already moving to adjust the press settings. "Now, let's see if we can turn you into a master counterfeiter before sunrise."

As they worked side by side, Tom marveled at Giselle's quick thinking and unwavering support. Despite the illegal nature of their activities, he felt a warmth in his chest. They were in this together, for better or worse.

"You know," Tom said, carefully aligning the next sheet of paper, "I never thought I'd say this, but I'm actually enjoying this bizarre little adventure with you."

Giselle grinned, her red hair catching the light. "Well, someone has to keep your life interesting, non? Now, let's make some money, Monsieur Beauchamp."

Tom's palms were slick with sweat as he stood in the dimly lit alley behind Joe's Pawn Shop. He clutched a brown paper bag containing a sampling of his freshly minted counterfeit bills, his heart pounding like a jackhammer.

"You got the goods?" a gruff voice called out from the shadows.

Tom cleared his throat, trying to sound more confident than he felt. "Depends. You got the cash?"

A burly man stepped into view, his eyes narrowing as he approached. "Let's see what you're peddling, old timer."

Tom's hand trembled slightly as he passed over the bag. The potential buyer, a rough-looking character with a scar across his left cheek, peered inside.

"These better be top-notch," the man growled, pulling out a bill and holding it up to the faint street light.

Tom's mind raced. What if he noticed the slight imperfection in the watermark? Or the barely perceptible difference in the paper texture?

The man's eyes widened suddenly. "Wait a minute... these ain't right!"

Panic surged through Tom's body. Without thinking, he blurted out, "Look! A three-headed dog!"

As the confused buyer instinctively turned to look, Tom snatched the bag and bolted down the alley, his legs pumping furiously.

"Hey! Get back here, you fraud!" the man's angry shouts echoed behind him.

Tom's breath came in ragged gasps as he zigzagged through the maze of back streets, his mind racing. This was not how he'd envisioned his first sale going.

After what felt like an eternity, Tom ducked into a quiet café, collapsing into a booth. As his heartbeat slowly returned to normal, he couldn't help but chuckle at the absurdity of his escape tactic.

"A three-headed dog? Really, Tom?" he muttered to himself, shaking his head. "You've got to come up with a better plan."

Determined to find a more reliable buyer, Tom spent the next few evenings cautiously exploring The Rusty Nail, a seedy bar known for its less-than-savory clientele. He nursed watered-down whiskey, straining to overhear snippets of conversation that might lead him to potential customers.

On his third night, Tom found himself inadvertently drawn into a heated argument about the merits of various heist movies.

"Ocean's Eleven? Please," Tom scoffed, surprising himself with his boldness. "The Italian Job is clearly superior."

A wiry man with a pencil-thin mustache turned to face him. "You sound like you know your stuff, friend. What's your game?"

Tom's mind raced. This could be his chance. "Let's just say I deal in... financial opportunities," he replied cryptically.

The man leaned in, intrigued. "Is that so? Maybe we should continue this conversation somewhere more private."

As they moved to a corner booth, Tom felt a mix of excitement and apprehension. He was finally making progress, but the stakes were higher than ever. One wrong move, and his dreams of easy money could turn into a nightmare of steel bars and orange jumpsuits.

"So," the mustached man said in a low voice, "what kind of 'opportunities' are we talking about?"

Tom leaned in, his heart racing as he lowered his voice. "Let's just say I've got access to some high-quality merchandise that could be very profitable for the right buyers." He patted his jacket pocket, feeling the crisp edges of a sample bill through the fabric.

The man's eyes lit up with interest. "I might know some people who'd be interested in such... merchandise. But first, I need to know I can trust you." He extended his hand. "Name's Jacques. And you are?"

"Tom," he replied, shaking Jacques' hand firmly. As their palms met, Tom noticed a small tattoo on Jacques' wrist - a stylized compass rose. Something about it nagged at the back of his mind, but he pushed the thought aside.

Over the next few weeks, Tom's operation expanded rapidly. Jacques introduced him to a network of buyers spanning several countries, each more eager than the last to get their hands on Tom's expertly crafted bills.

One evening, as Tom was preparing for a drop, Giselle's voice cut through his concentration. "Tom, have you noticed anything... off about these new buyers?"

He paused, raising an eyebrow. "Off how?"

Giselle bit her lip, her green eyes narrowing. "I've been doing some digging. That Jacques guy? His background doesn't add up. And I overheard him on the phone using some weird phrases. It sounded like... cop talk."

Tom's stomach dropped. "Cop talk? Are you sure?"

"Pretty sure," Giselle nodded, her red hair bobbing. "I think we might be dealing with an undercover operation."

Tom sank into a chair, his mind reeling. "If that's true, we're in deep trouble. But we can't just back out now. They'd get suspicious."

Giselle placed a comforting hand on his shoulder. "What are we going to do?"

Tom closed his eyes, taking a deep breath. When he opened them, there was a glint of determination. "We'll have to be extra careful. Maybe we can use this to our advantage somehow. We just need to stay one step ahead."

As they discussed their options, neither of them realized that the very man they were talking about, Jacques - whose real name was Marc-André Leblanc - was sitting in an unmarked car just down the street, listening intently to every word through a hidden microphone.

Tom's hands trembled slightly as he gripped the briefcase filled with counterfeit bills. The abandoned warehouse loomed before him, its rusty corrugated walls a stark reminder of the illicit nature of this meeting. He took a deep breath, steadying himself.

"Just another routine drop," he muttered, more to calm his nerves than anything else. "In and out, like always."

As he approached the entrance, a flicker of movement caught his eye. Tom froze, his heart racing. Was that a glint of metal behind those crates? He shook his head, trying to dispel the paranoia Giselle's suspicions had planted.

"Get it together, Beauchamp," he chided himself, pushing open the creaky door.

Inside, the air was thick with dust and tension. Tom's footsteps echoed ominously as he made his way to the center of the cavernous space. The buyer, a burly man with a thick mustache, emerged from the shadows.

"You're late," the man growled.

Tom forced a smile. "Traffic. You know how it is."

As they began the exchange, Tom couldn't shake the feeling that something was off. The hairs on the back of his neck stood up, and he found himself scanning the darkness, half-expecting to see the glint of handcuffs or the barrel of a gun.

Suddenly, a booming voice shattered the silence. "This is the police! You're surrounded!"

Tom's mind raced. He locked eyes with the buyer, who looked equally shocked. In that moment of confusion, Tom made a split-second decision. He hurled the briefcase at the approaching officers and bolted for the back exit.

"Halt!" shouted a voice behind him. Tom recognized it as Sergeant Jean-Guy Tremblay's gruff tone.

As he ran, Tom's foot caught on a loose board. He stumbled, arms windmilling comically as he tried to regain his balance. In his panic, he crashed into a stack of empty paint cans, sending them clattering across the floor in a cacophony of metallic thuds.

"Merde!" Tom cursed, scrambling to his feet. He could hear the heavy footsteps of the officers closing in.

With a burst of desperate energy, Tom spotted a small window high up on the wall. It was his only chance. He leaped onto a nearby crate, stretching his arms towards freedom. Just as his fingers grasped the windowsill, the crate wobbled beneath him.

"Oh no, no, no," Tom muttered, feeling himself losing balance.

In a final, graceless attempt, Tom launched himself through the window, tumbling head over heels onto a pile of soggy cardboard boxes outside. As he lay there, winded and covered in grime, he couldn't help but let out a hysterical laugh.

"Well, Giselle," he wheezed to himself, "I guess your hunch was right after all."

The sound of approaching sirens snapped Tom back to reality. With a groan, he picked himself up and hobbled away into the night, wondering how on earth he was going to explain this to Giselle.

Chapter 3

Tom's rusty sedan groaned to a halt outside the squat, gray building. He peered through the windshield, his eyes narrowing as he surveyed the empty parking lot. Perfect. Just as he'd planned.

With a grunt, he heaved himself out of the car, his joints protesting after the long drive. The cool evening air nipped at his cheeks as he popped the trunk, revealing a stack of cardboard boxes.

"Well, old girl," he muttered to the car, patting its dented fender, "looks like we're really doing this."

Tom hefted the first box, wincing at its weight. As he trudged towards the building, keys jangling in his pocket, he couldn't help but chuckle at the absurdity of it all. Here he was, Tom Beauchamp, former brake pad mogul, sneaking around like a cat burglar.

The lock clicked open, and Tom stepped into the musty darkness. He fumbled for the light switch, blinking as harsh fluorescents flickered to life. The room was bare save for a folding table and chair in the corner.

"Home sweet home," he quipped to the empty space.

Tom made quick work of unloading the car, his movements efficient despite his aching muscles. With each trip, the room filled with the tools of his new trade: a gleaming printing press, reams of specialized paper, inks of various hues.

As he arranged the equipment on the table, Tom's hands moved with practiced precision. He'd rehearsed this setup a hundred times in his garage, much to the bewilderment of his neighbors.

"Just a new hobby," he'd told Mrs. Goldstein when she'd inquired about the strange noises. If only she knew.

Tom paused, running his fingers over the smooth surface of the printing press. It was a beautiful machine, really. In another life, he might have appreciated it purely for its craftsmanship.

"You and me," he murmured to the press, "we're going to change everything."

With a deep breath, Tom reached for the first ream of paper. It was time to get to work.

Tom's fingers danced across the printing press controls, adjusting dials and levers with the precision of a master pianist. The familiar scent of ink filled his nostrils as he fine-tuned the settings, his brow furrowed in concentration.

"Just a hair to the left," he muttered, tweaking the alignment. "Perfect."

He stepped back, admiring the intricate setup. The press hummed softly, ready to breathe life into his audacious plan. Tom's heart raced with a mixture of excitement and apprehension.

"Well, old girl," he addressed the machine, "let's see if we can fool Uncle Sam."

As he fed the first sheet of paper into the press, Tom's mind wandered to the potential consequences of his actions. The rhythmic whir of the machine seemed to echo his conflicted thoughts.

"It's just a few bills," he reasoned aloud, his voice barely audible over the press. "How much damage could it really do?"

But even as the words left his lips, images of economic chaos flashed through his mind. He saw headlines decrying a flood of counterfeit cash, markets in turmoil, innocent people suffering.

Tom's hand hesitated over the start button. "Am I really prepared to shoulder this responsibility?" he wondered, his earlier bravado wavering.

The press continued its steady hum, waiting patiently for his decision. Tom closed his eyes, took a deep breath, and pressed the button. The machine sprang to life, churning out the first of many perfect replicas.

"No turning back now," he whispered, watching the crisp bills emerge. "For better or worse, Tom Beauchamp, you're in the counterfeiting business."

As the press whirred to life, Tom's mind took an unexpected detour into the realm of absurdity. He chuckled to himself, imagining the most ridiculous outcomes of his illicit endeavor.

"What if," he mused aloud, his eyes crinkling with amusement, "I accidentally print my own face on these bills instead of old Benjamin's?"

The mental image of his weathered, graying visage adorning a stack of twenties sent him into a fit of laughter. "I can see the headlines now," he continued, wiping a tear from his eye. "'Local Man Becomes Face of New Currency: Economy in Shambles!'"

Tom's laughter echoed through the empty room, a stark contrast to the serious nature of his actions. As his chuckles subsided, another outlandish scenario popped into his head.

"Or worse," he said, his tone mock-serious, "I could end up in some international spy thriller. Tom Beauchamp: Accidental Counterfeiter turned CIA Asset." He struck a dramatic pose, holding an imaginary gun. "The name's Beauchamp. Tom Beauchamp."

Despite the levity of his thoughts, a nagging doubt persisted in the back of his mind. Tom's smile faded as he turned back to the press, watching it churn out perfect replicas of U.S. currency.

He took a deep breath, squaring his shoulders. "Come on, Tom," he muttered, his voice taking on a more determined tone. "Eyes on the prize. This is your ticket to the good life."

Closing his eyes, Tom allowed himself to envision the future he'd been dreaming of. A comfortable retirement, free from financial worries. Maybe a beachfront property, or that classic car he'd always wanted.

"Just think," he said softly, a small smile playing on his lips, "No more 60-hour work weeks. No more stress about making ends meet."

He opened his eyes, gazing at the stacks of bills with renewed resolve. "This is my chance to finally live, not just survive."

With a determined nod, Tom refocused on his task. The doubts were still there, but for now, his ambition burned brighter. He had come too far to turn back now.

Tom's hands trembled slightly as he grasped the first sheet of specialized paper. He took a deep breath, steadying himself before carefully feeding it into the press. The machine whirred to life, its rhythmic hum filling the room as it began its work.

"Here goes nothing," Tom muttered, his eyes fixed on the paper's journey through the press. As the first counterfeit bill emerged, he gasped softly. The intricate designs and security features of a genuine U.S. dollar materialized before his eyes, eerily perfect in every detail.

"My God," he whispered, carefully lifting the bill to examine it. "It's... it's flawless."

The press continued its steady rhythm, churning out bill after bill. Tom's focus sharpened, his earlier doubts temporarily forgotten as he immersed himself in the process. He meticulously inspected each note, discarding any that showed even the slightest imperfection.

"Can't have any weak links in the chain," he murmured, his tone a mixture of pride and nervousness. "One sloppy bill could bring this whole house of cards tumbling down."

As he worked, the constant hum of the machinery became almost meditative. Tom found himself falling into a focused trance, his movements becoming more fluid and confident with each passing minute.

"You know," he said to himself, a wry smile playing on his lips, "I never thought I'd say this, but I think I might have missed my calling as a printer. Who knew all those years running a brake pad factory were just preparing me for a life of crime?"

As the hours ticked by, Tom watched with growing excitement as the stacks of counterfeit bills grew taller and taller. His eyes, once weary from years of mundane business, now sparkled with renewed vigor.

"Would you look at that," he breathed, running a hand through his graying hair. "It's like watching a fortune materialize out of thin air."

Tom's mind raced with possibilities. He paced the room, gesticulating as he spoke to himself. "No more pinching pennies, no more sleepless nights worrying about payroll. I could buy that beach house in Maui, travel the world..."

He paused, chuckling softly. "Hell, I could probably buy my own island if I wanted to."

The rhythmic hum of the printing press provided a steady backdrop to his daydreams. Tom's steps became more animated, almost bouncy, as he moved around the room.

"Imagine the look on Janet's face when I pull up in a brand new Porsche," he mused, a mischievous grin spreading across his face. "She always said I was too cautious with money. Well, darling, how's this for living large?"

Tom stopped in his tracks, taking a deep breath. He turned slowly, surveying the room with a sense of awe. Neat stacks of crisp twenties covered every available surface, the fruit of his months of painstaking research and preparation.

"My God," he whispered, his voice tinged with both pride and disbelief. "I really did it."

As Tom's eyes swept over the stacks of counterfeit bills, his elation began to waver. A knot formed in his stomach, and he felt his shoulders tense. He ran a hand over his face, suddenly feeling every one of his years.

"What am I doing?" he muttered, his voice barely audible over the hum of the printing press. "This isn't just some harmless prank. These bills... they could ruin people's lives."

He picked up one of the crisp twenties, examining it closely. "God, think of all the small businesses that could go under if they unknowingly accept these. The families that could lose everything."

Tom's mind raced with scenarios. He imagined a single mother, scraping by on minimum wage, unknowingly accepting one of his counterfeit bills as change. When she tried to use it to buy groceries for her kids, she'd be accused of passing fake currency. The thought made him feel sick.

"I'm not some Wall Street shark," he said, pacing nervously. "I'm just Tom Beauchamp, the brake pad guy. How did I end up here?"

He glanced at his reflection in the dusty window, barely recognizing the man staring back at him. "Is this really who I want to be?"

Just as quickly as the doubt had crept in, Tom shook his head, steeling himself. "No, no. I've come too far to back out now. Besides, it's not like I'm passing these out on street corners."

He straightened his shoulders, his voice growing firmer. "These are going straight to my contacts. Big players who know the risks. They'll handle the distribution. It's not my problem what happens after that."

Tom nodded to himself, his resolve strengthening. "I'm just the supplier. What they do with the product is their business. I'm minimizing the impact. Yeah, that's it."

He picked up another stack of bills, the weight of them reassuring in his hands. "This is my ticket out. My chance at a better life. I can't let a guilty conscience derail everything now."

Tom's hands moved with practiced efficiency as he carefully packed stacks of counterfeit bills into nondescript metal briefcases. The crisp scent of fresh ink lingered in the air, a constant reminder of the illicit nature of his work.

"Alright, let's see," he muttered, his brow furrowed in concentration. "That's $500,000 in each case. Five cases total. Two and a half million dollars. Not bad for a day's work, eh?"

He chuckled softly, but the sound was tinged with nervous energy. Tom's fingers traced the cool metal of a briefcase, his mind racing with possibilities.

"This is it," he whispered to himself. "My golden ticket. No more struggling to make ends meet. No more sleepless nights worrying about bills."

As he secured the latches on the final case, Tom felt a surge of pride mixed with trepidation. He straightened up, his back cracking from hours of hunched work.

"I've thought of everything," Tom said aloud, his voice echoing in the empty room. "The paper, the ink, the security features. Hell, I even nailed that weird plasticky smell real bills have."

He paced the length of the room, gesturing animatedly. "My buyers won't know what hit 'em. They'll be begging for more. And then… then I'll be set for life."

Tom paused, his hand resting on the stack of briefcases. A small voice in the back of his mind whispered doubts, but he pushed them aside.

"No turning back now, Tommy boy," he said firmly. "You've come too far. This is your moment."

With a deep breath, Tom squared his shoulders. His eyes, once weary, now sparkled with determination and a hint of mischief.

"Time to show the world what Tom Beauchamp can really do," he declared, a grin spreading across his face. "Look out, economy. Here I come."

Tom took one last sweeping look around the nondescript room, ensuring no trace of his illicit operation remained. His hand trembled slightly as he reached for the light switch, casting the space into darkness.

"Easy there, old boy," he muttered to himself, steadying his nerves. "Just another day at the office, right?"

As he stepped out into the crisp evening air, Tom couldn't help but chuckle at the absurdity of it all. Here he was, a former brake pad manufacturer turned counterfeiter, about to walk back into his mundane life as if nothing had changed.

He locked the door with a decisive click, then patted his pocket to double-check for the key. "Wouldn't that be a kicker," he mused aloud. "Master criminal foiled by forgetfulness. Film at eleven."

Tom's footsteps echoed on the empty sidewalk as he made his way to his car, a sensible sedan that screamed "nothing to see here." As he slid behind the wheel, a wave of exhaustion hit him.

"What have I gotten myself into?" he wondered, gripping the steering wheel tightly. The weight of his secret pressed down on him, making the familiar drive home feel surreal.

Yet, as he navigated the quiet streets, a spark of excitement ignited in his chest. "No more factory grime under my nails," he said, a smile tugging at his lips. "From now on, it's nothing but green ink and high living."

Tom pulled into his driveway, the same one he'd come home to for years. But tonight, everything felt different. As he stepped out of the car, he couldn't help but glance over his shoulder, half-expecting to see flashing red and blue lights.

"Get a grip, Tom," he admonished himself. "You're not in a crime thriller. You're just... redefining your career path."

With a deep breath, he walked towards his front door, ready to step back into his everyday life – all while carrying the weight of his extraordinary secret.

Chapter 4

The door creaked open, drawing Tom's attention from the worn leather armchair where he'd been anxiously fidgeting. A tall figure filled the doorway, casting a long shadow across the dimly lit room. Tom's breath caught in his throat as the man stepped inside, his presence immediately commanding the space.

"Mr. Beauchamp, I presume?" The newcomer's voice was as smooth as aged whiskey, carrying a hint of a European accent that Tom couldn't quite place.

Tom stood, his legs slightly unsteady. "Yes, that's me," he managed, extending his hand. "And you must be Mr. Dubois."

Patrice Dubois took Tom's hand in a firm grip, his piercing blue eyes seeming to look right through him. "Indeed, I am. It's a pleasure to make your acquaintance." His words rolled off his tongue with practiced ease, each syllable precisely enunciated.

Tom found himself transfixed by Patrice's appearance - the impeccably tailored suit, the salt-and-pepper hair groomed to perfection, the air of sophistication that seemed to emanate from every pore. This was a man who exuded confidence and power.

"Please, have a seat," Patrice gestured to the armchair Tom had vacated. "I trust you found the location without too much difficulty?"

Tom lowered himself back into the chair, his mind racing. This man was nothing like he'd imagined. He'd expected someone more... well, criminal-looking. But Patrice could have easily passed for a CEO or a diplomat.

"It was fine, thank you," Tom replied, trying to match Patrice's polished tone. "Your directions were quite explicit."

Patrice smiled, revealing perfect white teeth. "Excellent. I find that clarity in communication is paramount in our line of work, don't you agree?"

Tom nodded, feeling a bit out of his depth. "Absolutely," he said, hoping his voice didn't betray his nervousness.

As Patrice settled into the chair opposite him, Tom couldn't help but marvel at how surreal this all felt. Here he was, Tom Beauchamp, former brake pad factory owner, sitting across from a man who looked like he'd stepped out of a James Bond film. And they were about to discuss counterfeit money.

Life certainly had a way of taking unexpected turns.

Tom's fingers tapped a nervous rhythm on the armrest as he studied Patrice, searching for any sign of the criminal underbelly this man surely represented. Yet, all he saw was polished elegance. It was... unsettling.

"I must admit," Tom began, his voice careful and measured, "you're not quite what I expected, Mr. Dubois."

Patrice's eyebrow arched, a hint of amusement playing at the corners of his mouth. "And what did you expect, Mr. Beauchamp? A shifty-eyed miscreant skulking in the shadows?"

Tom felt heat creep up his neck. "Well, I... that is to say..."

"Perhaps a mustache-twirling villain?" Patrice continued, his eyes twinkling. "I do apologize for the lack of cape and top hat. I find they clash terribly with Armani."

Despite himself, Tom chuckled. The tension in his shoulders eased slightly. "I suppose I've watched too many crime dramas."

"Ah, but life is so much more interesting than fiction, wouldn't you agree?" Patrice leaned forward, his gaze intense. "After all, here you are – a respectable businessman venturing into uncharted waters. Now that's a plot twist worth exploring."

Tom shifted in his seat, both intrigued and wary. What exactly did this smooth-talking enigma have in store for him?

Patrice's blue eyes glinted with knowledge as he continued, "For instance, did you know that the global market for counterfeit currency is estimated to be worth over $70 billion annually? It's a fascinating ecosystem, really."

Tom's eyebrows shot up. "That's... more than I expected," he admitted, his curiosity piqued despite his reservations.

"Oh, it's just the tip of the iceberg," Patrice said, waving his hand dismissively. "The real intrigue lies in the interconnected web of players. From small-time operators to government-sanctioned operations, it's a delicate dance of economics, politics, and old-fashioned greed."

Tom leaned forward, his weariness momentarily forgotten. "Government-sanctioned? Surely you're joking."

Patrice's laugh was rich and warm. "My dear Tom, in this world, the line between legality and criminality is about as straight as a drunk man's walk home. Did you know that during World War II, the Nazis attempted to destabilize the British economy by flooding it with counterfeit pounds? Operation Bernhard, they called it. Quite the ambitious scheme."

"I had no idea," Tom murmured, genuinely fascinated.

"Ah, but here's where it gets truly amusing," Patrice said, his eyes twinkling with mischief. "Some of those same forgers later worked for the Israeli intelligence services. Talk about a career change, eh? From Nazi collaborators to Mossad assets. It's like a cosmic joke on morality."

Despite himself, Tom burst out laughing. "That's... that's absurd!"

"Welcome to the world of international finance, my friend," Patrice grinned. "Where today's villain might be tomorrow's hero, and everyone's just trying to stay ahead of the game."

As their laughter subsided, Tom found himself both amused and unsettled. Patrice's knowledge was impressive, but it also hinted at a depth of involvement that was slightly terrifying. What exactly had he gotten himself into?

Patrice leaned back in his chair, his piercing blue eyes fixed on Tom. "You know, Tom, you remind me of myself when I was younger. Full of potential, but held back by... shall we say, unnecessary scruples?"

Tom shifted uncomfortably, his fingers drumming on the armrest. "I wouldn't call them unnecessary," he muttered.

"Ah, but they are!" Patrice exclaimed, spreading his hands wide. "Look at where you are now. You've taken the first step into a larger world. Why stop there? The opportunities are endless, my friend."

Tom's brow furrowed. "I'm not sure I follow."

Patrice leaned forward, his voice dropping to a conspiratorial whisper. "Your ambition, Tom. It's admirable. But you're still thinking too small. With your skills, your meticulous planning... why limit yourself to this one venture? There are so many other avenues we could explore."

A cold tendril of unease coiled in Tom's stomach. "Other avenues?"

"Of course! Think bigger, Tom. International markets, cryptocurrency, even dabbling in some light insider trading. The risks may seem high, but I assure you, the rewards are... astronomical."

Tom's mind raced, images of wealth and success flashing before his eyes. But alongside them came visions of handcuffs, courtrooms, and prison cells. He swallowed hard, his throat suddenly dry.

"I... I don't know, Patrice. This was supposed to be a one-time thing. A chance to secure my future, not..."

"Not what? Not to truly live?" Patrice interrupted, his voice silky smooth. "You've spent your life playing by the rules, Tom. Where has it gotten you? A failed business and dashed dreams. It's time to take control of your destiny."

Tom's conscience screamed at him to refuse, to walk away. But a small voice in the back of his mind whispered of the possibilities. The comfort, the security, the respect that came with wealth. He found himself torn, caught between the man he'd always been and the man Patrice was urging him to become.

"I'll... I'll think about it," Tom finally managed, his voice barely above a whisper.

Patrice smiled, a predator sensing weakness in its prey. "That's all I ask, my friend. That's all I ask."

Patrice leaned back in his chair, his piercing blue eyes studying Tom with an intensity that made him squirm. "You know, Tom," he began, his refined accent lilting through the air, "in my line of work, I've found that the most successful men are those who can... adapt."

Tom furrowed his brow, curiosity getting the better of him. "Adapt? How do you mean?"

A enigmatic smile played on Patrice's lips. "Like a chameleon, my friend. One day, you're a respected businessman. The next, perhaps you're a daring entrepreneur in an emerging market. The key is to never let anyone truly know you."

Tom's mind reeled, trying to decipher Patrice's words. Was this advice or a warning? He cleared his throat, buying time to formulate a response. "That sounds... lonely."

Patrice chuckled, the sound both warm and chilling. "Lonely? Perhaps. But it's also liberating. Think about it, Tom. No expectations, no limitations. Just endless possibilities."

As Tom pondered this, Patrice rose smoothly from his seat, adjusting his impeccable suit. "Well, I'm afraid I must be going. Places to be, people to see, you understand."

Tom stood as well, feeling slightly dazed. "Of course, I-"

Patrice cut him off with a raised hand. "Before I go, let me leave you with this thought: In this game we play, Tom, the board is always changing. Make sure you're not left behind when the pieces move."

With that cryptic remark hanging in the air, Patrice strode towards the door. Tom watched him go, a mixture of fascination and unease swirling in his gut. What had he gotten himself into?

Tom's eyes followed Patrice's retreating figure, his mind a whirlpool of conflicting emotions. The tall man's confident stride and the soft click of his expensive shoes against the floor seemed to echo the tantalizing promises of wealth and success he'd dangled before Tom.

"Damn," Tom muttered under his breath, running a hand through his graying hair. He felt simultaneously exhilarated and terrified, like he was standing on the edge of a cliff, unsure whether to step back or leap into the unknown.

The room suddenly felt too small, too confining. Tom loosened his tie and moved to the window, pressing his forehead against the cool glass. The city sprawled before him, a maze of opportunities and pitfalls.

"What would Sarah think?" he wondered aloud, his wife's face flashing in his mind. He could almost hear her cautious voice, urging him to be careful, to consider the consequences.

But then Patrice's smooth, accented words slithered back into his thoughts. "No expectations, no limitations. Just endless possibilities."

Tom's reflection stared back at him, eyes filled with a mix of determination and doubt. "Is this really who I want to be?" he asked himself, his voice barely above a whisper.

He turned away from the window, his gaze falling on the briefcase Patrice had left behind. It sat there innocuously, but Tom knew it contained the keys to a world he'd only dreamed of entering.

With a deep sigh, he walked over to his desk and sank into the chair. "Okay, Tom," he said, straightening his shoulders. "Time to make a decision. What's the next move?"

As he reached for a pen and paper, ready to weigh his options, Tom couldn't shake the feeling that whatever choice he made, his life would never be the same again.

Chapter 5

Tom's heart raced as he stepped into the dimly lit warehouse. The musty scent of old paper and ink filled his nostrils, awakening a mix of excitement and trepidation within him. This was it—the moment he'd been meticulously planning for months.

"Welcome to your new office, Mr. Beauchamp," a gruff voice called out from the shadows.

Tom squinted, his eyes adjusting to the low light. "Thank you. I'm eager to get started."

As he moved further into the space, the silhouettes of printing presses loomed before him like hulking beasts. Tom ran his hand along the cool metal of the nearest machine, marveling at its intricate gears and levers.

"This beauty here is your new best friend," the voice continued, now accompanied by a stocky figure emerging from behind the press. "She'll teach you everything you need to know about intaglio printing."

Tom nodded, his mind already racing with possibilities. "I've done my research, but I'm sure there's no substitute for hands-on experience."

"You got that right," the man chuckled. "Let's see what you can do."

With a deep breath, Tom approached the press. His fingers trembled slightly as he reached for the specialized paper and ink. This is it, he thought. No turning back now.

As he began to set up the press, Tom's brow furrowed in concentration. He carefully poured the ink into the reservoir, his movements slow and deliberate.

"Steady hands are key," he muttered to himself. "Just like fixing those brake pads back in the day."

But as he tilted the ink bottle, his elbow knocked against the paper tray. In a heart-stopping moment, Tom watched in horror as the stack of pristine, expensive paper cascaded to the floor, right as the ink bottle slipped from his grasp.

"No, no, no!" Tom cried out, lunging to catch the falling bottle. But it was too late. Ink splattered across the floor, creating a Rorschach-like pattern on the scattered papers.

Tom stood frozen, his pants and shoes now speckled with black ink. He looked up at his instructor, his face a mix of embarrassment and dismay.

"Well," the man said, barely suppressing a grin, "I guess we can say you've made your mark on the industry already."

Tom couldn't help but let out a rueful chuckle. "Not exactly the first impression I was hoping to make."

As he bent down to start cleaning up the mess, Tom's mind raced. Is this a sign? Am I in over my head? But as he looked at the intricate design on one of the ink-stained papers, his resolve strengthened. No, he thought. This is just the beginning. I've come too far to give up now.

"Don't worry about it," the instructor said, handing Tom a rag. "Everyone makes mistakes at first. The key is to learn from them."

Tom nodded, a determined glint in his eye. "Absolutely. I'm here to learn, after all. And I won't let a little spilled ink stop me."

As he mopped up the inky mess, Tom couldn't help but smile at the absurdity of the situation. From respected businessman to amateur counterfeiter, covered in ink on his first day. It was a far cry from the glamorous life of crime he'd imagined, but he was just getting started. And Tom Beauchamp was nothing if not persistent.

Tom's brow furrowed as he carefully positioned the printing plate on the press. "This time," he muttered, his voice tinged with determination, "I'll get it right."

He lowered the press, feeling the satisfying resistance as metal met paper. But as he lifted it, his heart sank. The image on the paper was a jumbled mess, the intricate details of the twenty-dollar bill warped beyond recognition.

"Damn it!" Tom exclaimed, running a hand through his graying hair. He glanced at the instructor, who was watching with a mixture of amusement and sympathy. "I don't understand. What am I doing wrong?"

The instructor stepped closer, examining the plate. "Well, Mr. Beauchamp, for starters, your plate is upside down. Again."

Tom's cheeks flushed with embarrassment. "Of course it is," he sighed, shaking his head. "You'd think after running a factory, I'd be better at this kind of thing."

As he adjusted the plate, Tom's mind wandered. Is this really worth it? All this frustration, the risk? But then he thought of the comfortable life that awaited him if he succeeded, and his resolve hardened.

"Alright," Tom said, squaring his shoulders. "Let's try this again."

He carefully aligned the plate, double-checking its orientation. As he lowered the press, his hand slipped, causing him to apply too much pressure. When he lifted it, his eyes widened in horror.

There, in the middle of Andrew Jackson's forehead, was a perfect imprint of Tom's own thumbprint.

"Oh, for heaven's sake," Tom groaned, frantically grabbing a nearby cloth. He began rubbing at the bill, his movements growing more frenzied as the ink only smeared further. "This can't be happening."

The instructor couldn't contain his laughter any longer. "Well, Mr. Beauchamp, I think you've just created the world's most identifiable counterfeit bill. Congratulations!"

Tom looked up, his face a comical mask of despair and ink smudges. "I suppose this isn't quite the mark I was hoping to leave on the world of finance," he said dryly.

Tom sighed, setting aside the ruined bill and reaching for a fresh sheet of paper. "Third time's the charm, right?" he muttered, feeding it into the printer.

The machine whirred to life, but instead of smoothly accepting the paper, it made an ominous grinding noise. Tom's brow furrowed. "What now?" he groaned, leaning in to inspect the printer.

Suddenly, the paper crumpled inside with a sickening crunch. Tom's eyes widened in panic. "No, no, no!" He frantically reached for the paper, trying to tug it free. The printer responded by sucking in more paper, creating a messy accordion of half-printed bills inside its innards.

"Come on, you infernal contraption!" Tom grunted, wrestling with the machine. He yanked harder, and with a loud rip, a wad of mangled paper came free, sending Tom stumbling backward.

Regaining his balance, Tom stared at the mess in his hands. "Well, that's one way to make money disappear," he quipped dryly, tossing the ruined bills onto a growing pile beside him.

Determined not to be defeated, Tom turned back to the printer. "Alright, let's try this again," he said, his voice a mix of frustration and resolve. He carefully fed another sheet into the machine, holding his breath as it began to print.

For a moment, it seemed to be working. Then, with a sound like a dying cat, the printer jammed again.

"Oh, for the love of..." Tom muttered, diving back in. As he fought with the machine, his mind raced. I've got to get this right. There's too much riding on this to fail now.

After what felt like an eternity of paper cuts and ink stains, Tom finally managed to print a single, uncrumpled bill. Breathing heavily, he held it up to the light, squinting as he examined every detail.

"Now, let's see what we've got here," he murmured, pulling out a real twenty for comparison. His eyes darted back and forth between the two bills, searching for discrepancies.

Tom's eyes strained as he scrutinized every minute detail of the counterfeit bill. The longer he looked, the more his confidence wavered. He ran a hand through his graying hair, leaving a faint ink smudge on his forehead.

"What am I doing?" he whispered to himself, the weight of his actions suddenly pressing down on him. He slumped into a nearby chair, the bills still clutched in his hands.

"I'm a businessman, for crying out loud," Tom said aloud, his voice echoing in the empty room. "Not some... some criminal mastermind." He chuckled humorlessly at the thought.

His mind raced with potential consequences. Prison. Ruined reputation. His life's work - gone. Was it worth it?

"But then again," he mused, straightening up, "isn't this just another business venture? High risk, high reward?"

As Tom stood, ready to resume his work, his elbow knocked against an open bottle of ink. Time seemed to slow as he watched it topple, helpless to stop it.

"No, no, no!" he cried, but it was too late. The bottle upended, dousing him in a wave of black ink.

Tom stood frozen, dripping with ink from head to toe. He blinked, ink running down his face like macabre tears.

"Well," he said, his voice dripping with sarcasm, "I suppose this is one way to get into character."

He caught sight of himself in a nearby mirror and couldn't help but laugh at the absurdity of his appearance. "Look at me," he chuckled, "I'm a walking, talking counterfeit bill. Maybe I should just wrap myself in green paper and call it a day."

Tom's laughter subsided, replaced by a familiar spark of determination in his ink-stained eyes. He grabbed a nearby rag and began wiping his hands, leaving smudges of black across the fabric.

"Alright, Beauchamp," he muttered to himself, "you didn't come this far to let a little ink stop you. Time to get back to work."

With renewed vigor, Tom approached the printing press. His hands, still slightly slick with ink, trembled as he carefully aligned the printing plate.

"Steady now," he whispered, lowering the plate onto the specialized paper. The machine whirred to life, and Tom held his breath.

As the press rolled, Tom's eyes widened. The image emerging was crisper than his previous attempts, the lines more defined.

"Well, I'll be damned," he breathed, carefully lifting the freshly printed bill. He held it up to the light, scrutinizing every detail. "The shading on Franklin's face... it's actually starting to look right."

Tom's excitement grew as he printed another bill, then another. Each one showed subtle improvements - the colors more vibrant, the intricate patterns more accurate.

"It's like riding a bike," Tom mused, a small smile playing on his lips. "Once you get the hang of it..."

He paused, realizing the absurdity of comparing counterfeiting to cycling. "Though I suppose the consequences of falling are a bit more severe in this case," he added with a dry chuckle.

As the stack of increasingly convincing bills grew, Tom couldn't help but feel a mix of pride and unease. He ran his fingers over the textured surface of his latest creation, marveling at how close it felt to the real thing.

"I'm getting there," he murmured, his voice a mixture of awe and apprehension. "But at what cost?"

Tom's hands trembled slightly as he carefully loaded the final plate into the press. This was it - the culmination of days of frustration, ink-stained clothes, and countless ruined attempts. He took a deep breath, steadying himself.

"Alright, old girl," he muttered to the machine, patting it gently. "Let's make this one count."

The press hummed to life, and Tom watched with bated breath as it worked its magic. When it finally stopped, he gingerly lifted the paper, his heart pounding.

"Holy smokes," he whispered, holding the bill up to the light. Every detail was perfect - from the intricate filigree to the subtle color gradients. He allowed himself a small, satisfied smile. "We did it."

Tom's eyes crinkled as he admired his handiwork. "Franklin, my friend, I do believe we've just made you a twin."

As he set the flawless counterfeit aside, Tom's smile faded slightly. He glanced around the room, taking in the scattered evidence of his journey - crumpled bills, ink stains, and the faint smell of failure that had permeated the air for days.

"What a ride it's been," he mused, running a hand through his graying hair. "From brake pads to fake twenties. Mom would be so proud," he added with a wry chuckle.

Tom began tidying up, his movements deliberate and thoughtful. "I've come a long way since that first disaster," he reflected. "But am I really ready for what comes next?"

Tom was just about to power down the printer when his cell phone rang, startling him. He fumbled in his pocket, his heart racing as he glanced at the unfamiliar number on the screen.

"Hello?" he answered, his voice cautious.

"Is this Tom Beauchamp?" a gravelly voice asked.

Tom hesitated, his brow furrowing. "Who's asking?"

"Let's just say I'm an interested party," the voice replied. "Word on the street is you've been practicing a new... art form."

Tom's blood ran cold. He gripped the phone tighter, his knuckles turning white. "I'm afraid I don't know what you're talking about," he said, trying to keep his voice steady.

A low chuckle came through the line. "Oh, I think you do, Tom. And I have a proposition for you."

Tom's mind raced. How could anyone know? He'd been so careful. "I'm listening," he said cautiously, his free hand absently tracing the outline of the counterfeit bill in his pocket.

"Good," the voice purred. "Because this could be very lucrative for both of us. Meet me at the old warehouse on 5th and Main. Tomorrow, midnight."

The line went dead, leaving Tom standing in stunned silence. He slowly lowered the phone, his heart pounding in his ears.

"What have I gotten myself into?" he whispered to the empty room. The triumph of moments ago felt distant now, replaced by a gnawing fear in the pit of his stomach.

Tom glanced at the stack of perfect counterfeit bills, then back at his phone. He had a choice to make, and the clock was ticking.

Chapter 6

Tom's fingers drummed nervously on the kitchen table as Giselle poured her morning coffee. The aroma of fresh brew filled their small apartment, but it did little to calm his racing heart. He cleared his throat, causing Giselle to look up from her mug with a raised eyebrow.

"Giselle, ma chérie," Tom began, his voice measured and deliberate. "I've been doing some thinking about our future."

Giselle's green eyes sparkled with curiosity as she sat across from him. "Oh? What kind of thinking, mon amour?"

Tom leaned forward, his weathered hands clasped tightly. "I've found a way for us to have the life we've always dreamed of. A way to become wealthy overnight."

Giselle tilted her head, her red hair cascading over one shoulder. "Tom, you're being mysterious. What are you talking about?"

He took a deep breath, steeling himself. "We're going to print our own money."

The words hung in the air like a heavy fog. Giselle's eyes widened, her coffee mug frozen halfway to her lips. Tom pressed on, his voice gaining momentum.

"I've researched everything, Giselle. The paper, the ink, the printing process. With your artistic eye and my planning skills, we could create perfect replicas. We'd be set for life."

Giselle slowly set down her mug, her brow furrowing. "Tom, are you... are you talking about counterfeiting?"

He nodded, a mixture of excitement and apprehension coursing through him. "Think about it, Giselle. No more worrying about bills, no more penny-pinching. We could travel, buy a house, live the life we've always wanted."

Giselle stood up abruptly, pacing the small kitchen. Her accent thickened with emotion as she spoke. "But Tom, this is illegal. It's not just breaking the law, it's... it's printing lies. We'd be cheating everyone who accepts those bills."

Tom felt a knot forming in his stomach. He'd anticipated resistance, but seeing the concern etched on Giselle's face made his resolve waver. Still, he pressed on.

"I know it sounds risky, but I've thought it all through. We'll be careful, discreet. I need you with me on this, Giselle. Your support, your trust. We're a team, remember?"

Giselle stopped pacing, her eyes meeting Tom's. He could see the conflict raging within her, loyalty warring with morality. The tension in the room was palpable, like a taut rubber band ready to snap.

"Tom," she said softly, her voice tinged with disappointment. "How did we get here? When did our dreams become something we could only achieve through crime?"

The weight of her words hit Tom like a physical blow. He slumped in his chair, suddenly feeling every one of his years. The silence stretched between them, filled with unspoken fears and shattered illusions.

Tom leaned forward, his eyes pleading. "Giselle, I know it's not ideal, but think of the possibilities. We've worked hard our whole lives, and what do we have to show for it? This is our chance to finally get ahead."

Giselle's brow furrowed, her green eyes searching Tom's face. "But at what cost, Tom? Our freedom? Our integrity?"

Tom stood up, crossing the room to take Giselle's hands in his. The touch of her skin against his weathered palms felt like an anchor in a storm of uncertainty.

"I promise you, we'll be smart about this. We'll take every precaution. And just imagine - no more struggling to make ends meet. We could travel, help your family back in Quebec. All those dreams we've talked about? They could finally be real."

Giselle bit her lip, conflict evident in her expression. After a long moment, she sighed. "Okay, Tom. I'm in. But we need rules. Strict ones."

Tom's face lit up, relief washing over him. "Of course, absolutely. Whatever you say."

"First," Giselle said, a hint of amusement creeping into her voice, "no buying anything flashy. No sudden Ferraris or diamond necklaces."

Tom chuckled. "What, you mean I can't get that solid gold toilet I've always wanted?"

Giselle rolled her eyes, but a small smile tugged at her lips. "And no telling anyone. Not a soul. This stays between us."

"Agreed," Tom nodded solemnly. "What else?"

"We set a limit," Giselle insisted. "Once we reach it, we stop. No getting greedy."

As they continued their surprisingly lighthearted discussion of counterfeiting dos and don'ts, Tom felt a mix of excitement and trepidation. They were really doing this. For better or worse, their lives were about to change forever.

Tom hunched over his laptop, his graying hair illuminated by the screen's glow. Giselle peered over his shoulder, her red locks cascading beside his face as they scrolled through obscure online forums.

"Look at this one," Tom murmured, pointing to a cryptic post. "They're offering 'specialty art supplies for discerning craftsmen.' That's got to be code."

Giselle's green eyes narrowed. "How can you be sure?"

Tom's fingers flew across the keyboard, typing out a carefully worded response. "Trust me, I've been researching this for months. You learn to read between the lines."

As he hit send, Tom's stomach churned with a mix of excitement and apprehension. *What have I gotten us into?*

"We need to be careful," Giselle whispered, her Quebecois accent more pronounced in her worry. "What if it's a trap?"

Tom patted her hand reassuringly. "That's why we're using encrypted channels and false identities. Remember, we're just passionate artists looking for high-quality paper."

Giselle snorted. "Right, because all artists need paper that feels exactly like U.S. currency."

"Hey, don't knock our artistic vision," Tom quipped, his eyes crinkling with amusement despite the tension.

A ping from the laptop made them both jump. "They've responded," Tom said, leaning in closer. "They want to meet. Tomorrow night."

Giselle's breath caught. "So soon? Are we ready for this?"

Tom swallowed hard, his measured tone belying his nerves. "We have to be. This is our chance, Giselle. Our ticket to a better life."

As they prepared for the meeting, Tom couldn't shake the feeling that they were crossing a line they could never uncross. But the memory of years of struggle, of dreams deferred, steeled his resolve. There was no turning back now.

The rented warehouse on the outskirts of town loomed before them, a hulking silhouette against the fading twilight. Tom pulled up in their nondescript van, packed to the brim with carefully selected printing equipment.

"Well, this is it," Tom said, his voice a mixture of excitement and trepidation. "Our new home away from home."

Giselle peered out the window, her green eyes scanning the area. "It's... charming," she deadpanned, a hint of a smile playing on her lips.

As they began unloading, Tom couldn't help but marvel at the culmination of their efforts. Each piece of equipment represented hours of research, careful selection, and no small amount of risk. The high-quality printer, the specialized inks, the UV scanner – all essential components in their audacious plan.

"Careful with that one," Tom cautioned as Giselle hefted a box. "That's our ticket to the big leagues."

Giselle raised an eyebrow. "You mean our ticket to federal prison?"

Tom chuckled, though there was a nervous edge to it. "Always the optimist, aren't you?"

As they set up the equipment, Tom's mind raced with possibilities and potential pitfalls. He'd spent countless nights poring over every detail, but now that they were here, doubt began to creep in. What if he'd overlooked something crucial?

"Tom?" Giselle's voice snapped him back to reality. "Where do you want the UV light?"

"Oh, uh, over by the printing station," he replied, shaking off his concerns. "We'll need it for quality control."

As the last piece of equipment found its place, they stood back, surveying their handiwork. The warehouse had been transformed into a veritable counterfeiting studio.

"It's really happening, isn't it?" Giselle murmured, a mix of awe and apprehension in her voice.

Tom nodded, his throat suddenly dry. "Yeah, it is. Ready to make some money?"

With a deep breath, they approached the printer. Tom's hands trembled slightly as he loaded the specialized paper. This was the moment of truth.

"Here goes nothing," he muttered, hitting the print button.

The machine whirred to life, and Tom watched with bated breath as the first bill emerged. It was far from perfect, but it was a start.

"Well?" Giselle asked, peering over his shoulder.

Tom held up the bill, a grin spreading across his face despite his nerves. "Ladies and gentlemen, we are officially in business."

Tom's grin faded as he squinted at the freshly printed bill. Something wasn't quite right. "Giselle, does this look... off to you?"

Giselle leaned in, her brow furrowing. "The color seems a bit pale, non?" She plucked the bill from Tom's hand, holding it up to the light. "And the watermark is barely visible."

Tom ran a hand through his graying hair, frustration creeping into his voice. "Damn it. I thought we had the settings perfect."

As they fiddled with the printer's color balance, a series of mishaps ensued. Giselle accidentally bumped the ink cartridge, sending a spray of green across her crisp white shirt. Tom, in his haste to fix the problem, tripped over a power cord, unplugging the entire system.

"Tabarnac!" Giselle exclaimed, dabbing at her ruined shirt. "This is harder than I thought it would be."

Tom couldn't help but chuckle as he untangled himself from the cord. "Who knew being a criminal mastermind was so... messy?"

They spent the next few hours tweaking and adjusting, each attempt bringing them closer to perfection. By midnight, exhaustion had set in, but their spirits remained high.

"Look at this," Tom said, holding up their latest creation. "It's nearly indistinguishable from the real thing."

Giselle nodded, a mix of pride and trepidation in her eyes. "We're getting good at this, Tom. Maybe too good."

As days turned into weeks, they fell into a rhythm. Tom would arrive at dawn, meticulously checking each component before firing up the printer. Giselle would join him a few hours later, her keen eye scrutinizing every bill for imperfections.

"You know," Giselle mused one afternoon, carefully stacking a fresh batch of hundreds, "I never thought I'd say this, but I'm actually enjoying this work."

Tom glanced up from the printer, a wry smile on his face. "Careful now, we don't want to get too comfortable in our life of crime."

But he couldn't deny the growing sense of camaraderie between them. Each successful batch felt like a shared victory, a secret triumph known only to them.

As Tom watched Giselle expertly sort through the day's haul, he felt a surge of affection. "We make a good team, don't we?"

Giselle looked up, her green eyes twinkling. "The best, mon cher. The very best."

Tom surveyed the growing pile of counterfeit bills with a mixture of pride and apprehension. "We need a better system for storing all this," he said, running a hand through his graying hair. "Can't exactly keep it under the mattress, can we?"

Giselle chuckled, her red hair catching the light as she shook her head. "Non, unless we want to sleep on a very lumpy bed." She paused, her brow furrowing in thought. "What about a safe? Hidden behind one of these ugly paintings?"

Tom considered this, his eyes scanning the bare walls of their rented facility. "Not bad, but we need something more... creative. Something no one would think to look for."

As they brainstormed, Tom's mind raced with possibilities. He could feel the weight of their secret pressing down on him, the need for absolute discretion paramount.

"I've got it," Giselle exclaimed suddenly, her green eyes sparkling with excitement. "Remember that old filing cabinet in the corner? What if we modified it? False bottoms in the drawers, maybe even a hidden compartment behind it?"

Tom's face lit up. "Giselle, you're a genius! We'll hide it in plain sight."

They spent the next few hours meticulously organizing their counterfeit stash, creating an intricate system of hidden compartments within the seemingly ordinary filing cabinet.

As they worked, Tom couldn't help but marvel at how far they'd come. "You know," he said, carefully sliding a stack of bills into a false-bottomed drawer, "a year ago, I never would have imagined us doing this."

Giselle paused, a wry smile playing on her lips. "Life has a funny way of surprising us, non? Though I must admit, this is quite the adventure."

Tom chuckled, the sound tinged with a hint of nervousness. "Adventure is one word for it. Just remember, we can't breathe a word of this to anyone. Not even a hint."

"Of course," Giselle nodded solemnly. "Our little secret."

As they finished their work, Tom stepped back to admire their handiwork. The filing cabinet looked completely ordinary, betraying nothing of the fortune hidden within.

"I think this calls for a celebration," he announced, pulling out a bottle of champagne he'd been saving for just such an occasion.

Giselle's eyes widened in surprise. "Tom Beauchamp, you old romantic!"

As they clinked their glasses together, Tom felt a surge of emotion. "To us," he said softly, "and to new beginnings."

Giselle's smile was radiant. "To us," she echoed, "and to whatever comes next."

Tom set down his champagne flute, his expression shifting from celebratory to serious. "Speaking of what comes next," he said, running a hand through his graying hair, "we need to talk strategy."

Giselle leaned forward, her green eyes sparkling with curiosity. "What did you have in mind, mon chéri?"

Tom moved to the small desk in the corner, pulling out a notepad. "We've got the product, now we need buyers," he explained, his tone measured and deliberate. "I've been doing some research on potential... let's call them 'distribution channels.'"

Giselle raised an eyebrow, a mix of intrigue and concern crossing her delicate features. "And what did you find?"

As Tom began to outline his ideas, Giselle listened intently, occasionally interjecting with questions or suggestions. The air in the room crackled with a palpable energy - part excitement, part nervousness.

"What about casino contacts?" Giselle suggested, twirling a lock of her vibrant red hair. "They deal with large amounts of cash daily."

Tom's eyes lit up. "Brilliant idea! We'll need to be careful, of course, but that could be a goldmine."

As they continued brainstorming, Tom felt a surge of anticipation coursing through his veins. This was it - the moment everything changed. He glanced at Giselle, her face animated as she spoke, and felt a wave of gratitude for her unwavering support.

"You know," he said softly, interrupting her mid-sentence, "I couldn't do this without you."

Giselle's expression softened, a warm smile spreading across her face. "We're in this together, Tom. Always."

As the evening wore on, their plans took shape, each idea bringing them closer to their goal. Tom's mind raced with possibilities, both thrilling and terrifying. Whatever the future held, he knew one thing for certain - life would never be the same again.

Chapter 7

Tom Beauchamp stood in his dimly lit basement, his eyes gleaming with pride as he gazed upon the neatly stacked pile of counterfeit twenty-dollar bills before him. The crisp edges and vibrant green hues of the freshly printed currency seemed to glow under the fluorescent light, a testament to his meticulous craftsmanship.

"Well, I'll be damned," Tom muttered to himself, running his fingers along the edge of a bill. "They're perfect."

He picked up a stack, fanning it out like a deck of cards. The familiar face of Andrew Jackson stared back at him from multiple angles, each portrait an exact replica of the genuine article. Tom's heart raced with excitement, the thrill of success coursing through his veins.

"This is it," he said, his voice barely above a whisper. "This is my ticket to a better life."

Tom's mind raced with possibilities. He imagined himself lounging on a beach, sipping a cold drink, far away from the stress and monotony of his former life as a brake pad factory owner. The counterfeit bills represented freedom, a chance to break free from the shackles of his mundane existence.

But as quickly as the excitement had come, it began to fade. Tom's brow furrowed as a sobering thought crossed his mind. "Now comes the hard part," he sighed, setting the stack back down on the table.

He began to pace the small basement, his footsteps echoing off the concrete walls. "Who in their right mind is going to buy these without asking questions?" Tom wondered aloud, running a hand through his graying hair.

The reality of his situation settled in like a heavy weight on his shoulders. Creating the counterfeit bills had been the easy part; selling them without raising suspicion was an entirely different challenge.

Tom's mind raced, considering potential buyers. "The local businesses are out," he mused, tapping his chin thoughtfully. "Too risky. They'd spot a fake in a heartbeat."

He continued his pacing, each step bringing a new idea and a subsequent dismissal. "Maybe I could... no, that won't work. Or perhaps... no, too obvious."

Frustration began to bubble up inside him. Tom had spent months planning this operation, carefully researching and perfecting his counterfeiting technique. He hadn't considered that finding buyers would be such a daunting task.

"Come on, Tom," he chided himself. "You didn't come this far to give up now. Think!"

He closed his eyes, taking a deep breath to calm his racing thoughts. When he opened them again, his gaze fell on an old newspaper clipping pinned to the wall. It was an article about a local flea market, known for its eclectic mix of vendors and cash-only transactions.

A slow smile spread across Tom's face as an idea began to form. "Now that," he said, pointing at the clipping, "that just might work."

With renewed enthusiasm, Tom began to formulate a plan. The flea market could be the perfect place to introduce his counterfeit bills into circulation. Cash transactions, busy crowds, and vendors more concerned with making a sale than scrutinizing every bill – it was an ideal environment for his purposes.

As he continued to brainstorm, Tom felt a mix of excitement and apprehension. He knew the risks were high, but the potential payoff was too great to ignore. This was his chance to change his life, and he was determined to see it through, no matter the obstacles.

"One step at a time, old boy," Tom murmured to himself, his eyes once again drawn to the stack of counterfeit bills. "One step at a time."

Tom's fingers drummed nervously on the steering wheel as he pulled into the parking lot of Moe's Diner. The neon sign flickered weakly in the fading daylight, casting an eerie glow on the cracked asphalt. He spotted a lone figure hunched over a cup of coffee through the grimy window and took a deep breath.

"This is it," he muttered, straightening his tie. "Don't mess this up, Tom."

As he pushed open the diner's door, a bell jangled overhead. The potential buyer – a stocky man with a receding hairline – looked up, his eyes narrowing.

"You Beauchamp?" the man grunted.

Tom nodded, sliding into the booth across from him. "And you must be Mr. Johnson. I appreciate you meeting me on such short notice."

Johnson grunted again, pushing aside his coffee mug. "Let's cut to the chase. You got the goods?"

Tom's heart raced as he reached into his briefcase, pulling out a small stack of crisp twenties. "As promised. Top quality, just as we discussed."

Johnson's meaty hands snatched the bills, holding them up to the light. His brow furrowed as he examined them closely. "Where'd you say you got these from again?"

Tom's mouth went dry. He hadn't prepared for this question. "Oh, you know," he said, trying to keep his voice steady, "I have my sources. Discretion is key in this business, wouldn't you agree?"

Johnson's eyes narrowed further. "Uh-huh. And these sources, they're reliable? Because these bills... something seems off."

Tom felt a bead of sweat forming on his brow. He forced a chuckle, hoping it didn't sound as nervous as he felt. "I can assure you, Mr. Johnson, these bills are of the highest quality. Perhaps the lighting in here isn't ideal for—"

"The lighting's fine," Johnson cut him off, his voice gruff. "What I want to know is how you're getting your hands on bills this crisp. They almost look too perfect, if you catch my drift."

Tom's mind raced, searching for a plausible explanation. He couldn't let this deal fall through – not when he was so close to success.

Tom's fingers tapped nervously on his thigh, hidden beneath the table. He cleared his throat, buying himself a moment to think. "Well, Mr. Johnson, as I mentioned, my sources are confidential. But I can assure you that—"

"Confidential, my ass," Johnson growled, leaning forward. "These bills look fresh off the press. You're not running some kind of operation yourself, are you?"

Tom's heart hammered in his chest. He could feel the walls closing in, his carefully constructed plan crumbling before his eyes. *Think, Tom, think!* he urged himself silently.

"Now, now, let's not jump to conclusions," Tom said, forcing a smile that felt more like a grimace. He reached for his coffee cup, his hand trembling slightly. "Perhaps we could discuss this over a fresh cup of—"

In that moment, whether by divine intervention or sheer clumsiness born of panic, Tom's elbow caught the edge of his cup. Coffee erupted across the table, splattering onto Johnson's shirt and the bills in his hand.

"Oh, good heavens!" Tom exclaimed, jumping to his feet. "I'm so terribly sorry! Let me get some napkins!"

As he fumbled for the napkin dispenser, knocking it over in his haste, Tom's mind raced. This unexpected chaos might just be the lifeline he needed to salvage the situation.

As Johnson sputtered and cursed, dabbing at his shirt with a handful of napkins, Tom's eyes darted to the stack of counterfeit twenties. With a subtle movement, he slid his hand beneath the table, fingers grazing the smooth leather of his messenger bag.

"Here, let me help you with that," Giselle chimed in, her voice as smooth as honey. She leaned across the table, strategically blocking Johnson's view.

Tom seized the moment. His heart pounding, he swiftly swept the bills into his bag, the soft rustle of paper barely audible over Johnson's grumbling.

"This is a disaster," Tom lamented, his voice tinged with exaggerated dismay. "We should get this cleaned up properly. Giselle, dear, perhaps we should fetch the staff?"

Giselle's eyes met his, a flicker of understanding passing between them. "Of course, Tom. We wouldn't want to leave such a mess."

As they rose from their seats, Tom's mind raced. *We're not out of the woods yet,* he thought. *But if we play this right...*

"Mr. Johnson," Tom said, his tone apologetic yet firm, "I'm terribly sorry about this unfortunate incident. Why don't you get yourself cleaned up, and we'll reconvene once this mess is sorted?"

Johnson glowered, still dabbing at his shirt. "Fine," he growled. "But don't think this discussion is over, Beauchamp."

Tom nodded solemnly, guiding Giselle towards the exit. "Wouldn't dream of it. We'll be right back with help."

As they walked away, Tom leaned in close to Giselle, whispering, "Quick thinking back there, love. Now, let's make ourselves scarce before he realizes what's missing."

Giselle squeezed his arm, her voice low. "My heart's racing, Tom. Do you think he suspects?"

"Let's not stick around to find out," Tom murmured, quickening his pace.

As they made their way across the crowded hotel lobby, Tom's eyes darted nervously from side to side. His heart pounded in his chest, the weight of the counterfeit bills in his bag feeling heavier with each step.

"Excuse us," Giselle chirped, her voice unnaturally high as she sidestepped a waiter carrying a tray of champagne flutes. The waiter stumbled, and Tom instinctively reached out to steady him, nearly losing his grip on the bag.

"Careful there, friend," Tom said, his voice strained. *Keep it together, Beauchamp,* he chided himself.

Just then, a boisterous group of tourists burst through the revolving door, their laughter echoing through the lobby. Tom and Giselle found themselves caught in the middle, jostled from all sides.

"Tom!" Giselle yelped as she was pushed against a potted plant. "A little help?"

Tom reached for her hand, but in his haste, he tripped over someone's suitcase. He stumbled forward, narrowly avoiding a face-plant into a nearby fountain.

"Sorry, so sorry," he muttered, regaining his balance. *This is turning into a bloody circus,* he thought, exasperated.

As they neared the exit, Tom's eyes widened in horror. "Giselle," he hissed, "is that Johnson by the door?"

Giselle peered ahead, her green eyes narrowing. "No, it's just a bellhop. Breathe, Tom."

Finally, they pushed through the revolving door, the cool evening air washing over them. Tom inhaled deeply, his shoulders sagging with relief.

"We did it," he whispered, a hint of disbelief in his voice. "We actually did it."

Giselle leaned against him, her laughter tinged with nervous energy. "I thought that plant was going to eat me alive back there."

Tom chuckled, wrapping an arm around her. "Well, my dear, it seems we've survived another close call. What do you say we find somewhere a bit less... eventful to catch our breath?"

As they walked away from the hotel, Tom couldn't shake the feeling that their adventure was far from over. But for now, the weight of the bag at his side reminded him that they were one step closer to their dreams – however precarious that step might be.

Tom's laughter bubbled up from deep in his chest, a mixture of relief and adrenaline. He squeezed Giselle's shoulder, his eyes crinkling with mirth.

"Did you see that potential buyer's face when I 'accidentally' spilled my coffee?" Tom chuckled, his voice low. "I thought his eyes were going to pop right out of his head!"

Giselle snorted, her red hair bouncing as she shook with laughter. "Oh, mon dieu! And the way you fumbled with those napkins? Oscar-worthy performance, mon chéri."

Tom grinned, basking in their shared moment of triumph. But as they walked, his expression sobered. "We can't keep relying on dumb luck and impromptu magic tricks, though. We need a better strategy."

Giselle nodded, her green eyes sparkling with curiosity. "What are you thinking, Tom?"

He furrowed his brow, years of business experience kicking in. "We need to diversify. Spread the risk. Maybe... smaller transactions, multiple buyers?"

"Ooh, like a franchise?" Giselle quipped, earning a playful eye-roll from Tom.

"Not exactly, but... wait." Tom paused, an idea forming. "What about that friend of yours, the one who runs the laundromat?"

Giselle's eyes widened. "Pierre? You think he'd be interested?"

Tom shrugged, his mind racing. "It's worth a shot. Cash-heavy business, always need change..."

As they continued down the street, the cool night air filled with possibilities and the faint scent of danger, Tom couldn't help but feel a familiar thrill. This was just the beginning.

Tom squared his shoulders, his stride purposeful as they made their way down the dimly lit street. The weight of the counterfeit bills in his bag felt both exhilarating and terrifying.

"You know, Giselle," he said, his voice low and measured, "we're really stepping into uncharted territory here. Are you sure you're ready for this?"

Giselle's green eyes flashed with determination. "Tom, mon cher, I didn't come this far to back out now. We're in this together, remember?"

He nodded, a small smile tugging at his lips. "I know. I just... I can't help but think about what could go wrong."

As they passed under a flickering streetlight, Tom caught Giselle's gaze. In that moment, no words were needed. The gravity of their situation, the risks they were taking, it was all there in that shared look.

Giselle reached out and squeezed his hand. "We've come too far to turn back now, non? Besides," she added with a mischievous grin, "think of all the brake pads we won't have to sell."

Tom chuckled despite himself. "Fair point. Though I never thought I'd say this, but brake pads seem a lot less risky right now."

As they walked, Tom's mind raced with possibilities and potential pitfalls. The thrill of their narrow escape was fading, replaced by a steely resolve. They had to be smarter, more careful. No more close calls.

"You're right about Pierre," Giselle mused, breaking into his thoughts. "He's always complaining about the banks and their fees. This could be a win-win."

Tom nodded, his business instincts kicking in. "We'll need to approach him carefully. Maybe start small, test the waters."

As they turned the corner, the bustling nightlife of the city enveloped them. Tom felt a surge of determination. They were on the precipice of something big, something that could change their lives forever. The risks were enormous, but so were the potential rewards.

Giselle's laugh rang out, bright and clear against the city's din. "Oh, Tom! The look on your face when you spilled that coffee. I thought you were going to have a heart attack right there!"

Tom grinned, his weariness momentarily forgotten. "Hey, it worked, didn't it? Sometimes the best plans are the ones you make up on the spot."

They weaved through the evening crowd, the sidewalk a river of hurried pedestrians and glowing shop windows. Tom's hand instinctively patted his bag, feeling the reassuring bulk of their illicit cargo.

"So, what's our next move, mon cher?" Giselle asked, her green eyes sparkling with curiosity and excitement.

Tom's brow furrowed in concentration. "We need to spread out, minimize risk. Maybe hit up some of those mom-and-pop shops on Saint-Catherine Street. They're always strapped for cash."

As they passed a street performer juggling flaming batons, Giselle clapped in delight. "Ooh, like a scavenger hunt, but with fake money!"

"Exactly," Tom chuckled, marveling at her ability to find joy in even the most precarious situations. "But remember, we've got to be careful. No more close calls like today."

They turned down a quieter side street, the sounds of the city fading slightly. Tom felt a mix of exhilaration and anxiety bubbling in his chest. This was it - their big gamble, their shot at a better life. As they disappeared into the night, their laughter echoed off the brick buildings, a soundtrack to their daring adventure.

Chapter 8

The stench of stale beer and cigarette smoke assaulted Tom's nostrils as he pushed open the heavy wooden door of The Rusty Nail. A haze of smoke hung in the air, illuminated by the dim glow of neon beer signs and a few scattered overhead lamps. Tom's eyes watered slightly as he blinked, adjusting to the murky atmosphere.

"Well, this is certainly a step down from the country club," Tom muttered under his breath, straightening his slightly rumpled suit jacket. He made his way to the bar, his polished oxfords sticking slightly to the grimy floor with each step.

The bartender, a burly man with tattoos snaking up both arms, gave Tom a suspicious once-over. "What'll it be?"

"Scotch, neat," Tom replied, his voice steady despite the nervous flutter in his stomach. As the bartender poured his drink, Tom's eyes darted around the room, taking in the motley assortment of patrons.

A group of leather-clad bikers huddled around a pool table, their raucous laughter punctuating the low hum of conversation. In a dark corner booth, a man in a pinstriped suit leaned in close to a woman wearing far too much makeup, their hushed whispers barely audible.

Tom's fingers tapped an anxious rhythm on the sticky bar top as he scanned the faces, searching for any sign of a potential buyer or informant. "Come on, Tom," he thought to himself, "you didn't spend months planning this just to chicken out now. There's got to be someone here who can point you in the right direction."

A loud crash from the far end of the bar made Tom jump, nearly spilling his drink. He turned to see a heavily tattooed man sprawled on the floor, having apparently lost his battle with gravity and his bar stool.

"Hey, watch it!" the bartender bellowed, leaning over the bar to glare at the fallen patron. "You break it, you bought it, Joey!"

Tom couldn't help but chuckle, the tension in his shoulders easing slightly. As he turned back to his drink, he caught the eye of a well-dressed man seated a few stools down. The man raised an eyebrow, a knowing smirk playing at the corners of his mouth.

"First time here?" the man asked, his voice smooth as silk.

Tom hesitated for a moment before replying, "Is it that obvious?"

The man chuckled, sliding onto the stool next to Tom. "Let's just say you stick out like a sore thumb in that suit. I'm curious what brings a man like you to a place like this."

Tom's heart raced as he considered his response. This could be the opening he'd been looking for, but he had to play it cool. "Oh, you know," he said, forcing a casual shrug, "sometimes a man just needs a change of scenery. And who knows? Maybe I'm looking to make some new... business connections."

The man's eyes glinted with interest. "Is that so? Well, my friend, you might just be in luck. The name's Marcus. What say we grab a booth and discuss what kind of... business you might be interested in?"

As Tom followed Marcus to a secluded booth, he couldn't help but feel a mix of excitement and trepidation. "This is it," he thought, his palms slightly sweaty. "No turning back now. Time to see if all that research pays off."

Tom settled into the cracked leather booth, his eyes darting nervously around the dimly lit bar. Marcus slid in across from him, flanked by two burly men who looked like they ate nails for breakfast.

"So, stranger," Marcus leaned in, his voice barely above a whisper, "what kind of business are you looking to get into?"

Tom's mind raced, searching for the right words. He cleared his throat, trying to sound more confident than he felt. "Well, I've always been interested in... alternative revenue streams. Something with a high return on investment, if you catch my drift."

Marcus's eyes narrowed, studying Tom's face. "Is that so? And what makes you think we'd be interested in your... investment opportunities?"

Tom's heart pounded in his chest. This was it - sink or swim. He leaned in closer, lowering his voice. "Let's just say I've got access to some high-quality merchandise. The kind that could make a lot of people very happy... and very rich."

As the words left his mouth, Tom caught a snippet of conversation from the next booth. "...biggest score yet. Easy money, I'm telling you."

His ears perked up, but he kept his eyes locked on Marcus, who was now grinning like a shark that had just spotted its prey.

"Well, well," Marcus chuckled, "looks like we might have something to talk about after all. Why don't you tell me more about this merchandise of yours?"

Tom took a deep breath, steeling himself for what was to come. "This is it," he thought, "no turning back now. Time to see if all that careful planning was worth it."

Tom leaned in, his voice barely above a whisper. "Let's just say I've got connections in the printing business. High-quality stuff that even the experts have trouble spotting." He tapped his temple knowingly, a sly smile playing on his lips.

Marcus raised an eyebrow, intrigued. "That so? And what makes you think we'd be interested in such... delicate merchandise?"

Tom's mind raced, carefully choosing his next words. "Well, gentlemen, I couldn't help but overhear talk of 'big scores.' Thought maybe we could help each other out."

The group exchanged glances, a mix of suspicion and curiosity on their faces. Tom's heart hammered in his chest, but he kept his expression calm and confident.

Finally, a stocky man with a thick beard spoke up. "Alright, hotshot. You've got our attention. But how do we know you're not some Fed trying to set us up?"

Tom chuckled, the sound surprisingly genuine despite his nerves. "Me? A Fed? Fellas, I'm just a businessman looking to diversify my portfolio. Besides," he added with a wink, "do I look like I could run more than a block in these loafers?"

The group erupted in laughter, the tension visibly easing. Tom allowed himself a small sigh of relief, thinking, "That's it, Tom. Keep it light, keep them laughing. You've got this."

As the laughter died down, Marcus leaned back, a newfound respect in his eyes. "Alright, funny man. Why don't you tell us a bit more about these 'business ventures' of yours?"

Tom settled in, his posture relaxing as he prepared to spin the tale he'd meticulously crafted. All those nights of research were about to pay off. He just hoped his conscience could handle what came next.

As Tom finished regaling the group with his carefully constructed tale of small-time fraud and petty theft, a burly man with arms like tree trunks leaned forward, his interest piqued. His massive frame seemed to dwarf the rickety bar stool beneath him.

"You've got some brass ones, Tom," the man rumbled, a crooked grin spreading across his face. "Name's Tony. I think I might have something that'd interest a man of your... talents."

Tom's pulse quickened, but he kept his expression neutral. "Oh yeah? I'm all ears, Tony."

Tony's voice dropped to a conspiratorial whisper. "Got a contact who's always on the lookout for quality merchandise, if you catch my drift. Specializes in paper with presidents' faces on 'em."

Tom's eyes widened, feigning surprise and excitement. "Now that's what I call a golden opportunity," he chuckled, his mind racing. This was it - the break he'd been waiting for.

"I could set up a meet," Tony offered, his meaty hand clasping Tom's shoulder. "What do you say?"

Tom pretended to consider for a moment, all while his brain furiously catalogued every detail. The dim bar lights, the acrid smell of stale cigarettes, Tony's eager expression - all of it burned into his memory.

"Why not?" Tom finally replied, flashing a roguish grin. "After all, fortune favors the bold, right?"

As Tony began outlining the details, Tom's hand casually drifted to his pocket, fingertips brushing against the small notepad hidden there. He'd need every scrap of information for what came next.

'Keep it cool, Tom,' he thought to himself. 'You're in the thick of it now. No turning back.'

Tony led Tom through the smoky haze of the bar, weaving between rickety tables and patrons hunched over their drinks. They approached a dimly lit corner booth where a woman sat, her silhouette barely visible in the shadows.

"Sofia," Tony grunted, "Got someone you might want to meet."

As Tom slid into the booth, he caught his first glimpse of Sofia. She was striking, with sharp features and eyes that seemed to pierce right through him. Tom felt a bead of sweat form on his brow.

"Well, well," Sofia drawled, her voice husky. "What have we here? Another one of your strays, Tony?"

Tom chuckled, his mind racing to craft the perfect response. "Oh, I'm no stray. Just a businessman looking for... alternative investment opportunities."

Sofia's eyebrow arched. "Is that so? And what makes you think you're cut out for our line of work?"

Tom leaned back, affecting a casual air despite his racing heart. "Let's just say I've got a knack for turning paper into gold."

"Cute," Sofia smirked. "But it takes more than clever wordplay to make it in this game. Tell me, hotshot, what's the difference between intaglio and offset printing?"

Tom's extensive research kicked in. "Well," he began, his tone measured and confident, "intaglio involves etching the design into a metal plate, while offset uses a flat surface. Intaglio's preferred for its detail and security features, but offset's more cost-effective for large runs."

Sofia's eyes narrowed, a flicker of surprise crossing her face. "Not bad. But let's see how you handle this one..."

As Sofia fired off increasingly technical questions, Tom's mind whirred. He'd spent countless nights poring over counterfeiting techniques, and now it was paying off. With each correct answer, he could see Sofia's skepticism slowly melting away.

'Keep it together,' Tom thought, maintaining his facade of casual expertise. 'You've come too far to slip up now.'

Sofia leaned back, her eyes gleaming with newfound interest. "Well, well. It seems you know your stuff, Mr...?"

"Beauchamp," Tom replied, extending his hand. "Tom Beauchamp."

As they shook hands, Tom could feel the shift in the air. He'd passed her test, and now it was time to seal the deal.

"So, Ms. Sofia," Tom said, his voice low and steady, "I believe we both have something the other wants. Shall we discuss numbers?"

Sofia's lips curled into a sly smile. "I'm listening."

Tom's mind raced, calculating risks and rewards. "Let's start with, say, $500,000 worth. Quality guaranteed, of course."

"Bold," Sofia chuckled. "I like that. But how do I know I can trust you?"

Tom leaned in, his eyes locked on hers. "Trust is earned. I'm willing to start small if it means building a long-term partnership."

Sofia nodded slowly, considering his words. "Alright, Tom. Let's start with $100,000. If it's as good as you say, we can discuss larger amounts."

"Deal," Tom said, trying to contain his excitement. They exchanged burner phone numbers, agreeing to meet in a week to finalize the details.

As Tom stood to leave, he felt a mix of exhilaration and trepidation. 'Remember,' he thought, 'these aren't friends. Stay sharp.'

"It's been a pleasure," Tom said, nodding to Sofia and Tony. "I look forward to our future... ventures."

As he navigated through the smoky bar, Tom's mind buzzed with possibilities. 'This is it,' he thought, his heart racing. 'The big break I've been waiting for.'

The cool night air hit Tom's face as he stepped out of the bar, a welcome respite from the stuffy atmosphere inside. He leaned against the brick wall, his breath visible in the chilly air, and closed his eyes for a moment.

"Christ," he muttered, running a hand through his graying hair. "What have I gotten myself into?"

Tom's mind raced, replaying the conversation with Sofia. He'd done it—he'd actually secured a deal. The thrill of success mingled with a gnawing anxiety in his gut.

"One step at a time, Beauchamp," he told himself, his voice barely above a whisper. "You've come too far to back out now."

A cat yowled in a nearby alley, startling Tom. He chuckled nervously, realizing how on edge he was. As he pushed off the wall and started walking towards his car, he began mentally cataloging his next moves.

"Okay, so I've got a week to get everything in order," he mused aloud, his footsteps echoing in the empty street. "Gotta make sure the bills are perfect. Can't afford any slip-ups now."

Reaching his car, Tom paused, his hand on the door handle. He looked back at the bar, its neon sign flickering weakly in the darkness.

"This is it, old boy," he said to his reflection in the car window. "No turning back now."

With a deep breath, Tom opened the door and slid into the driver's seat. As he started the engine, a wry smile played on his lips.

"Who would've thought," he chuckled, shaking his head, "that selling brake pads would lead to this?"

Tom pulled away from the curb, his mind already racing with plans and contingencies. The path ahead was uncertain, fraught with danger, but for the first time in years, Tom felt truly alive.

Tom eased his car onto the nearly empty streets, the hum of the engine a soothing counterpoint to his racing thoughts. Streetlights cast intermittent shadows across his face, highlighting the lines of tension around his eyes.

"Well, Tom," he muttered to himself, fingers drumming on the steering wheel, "you wanted excitement. Looks like you've found it in spades."

He couldn't help but let out a dry chuckle, the sound filling the car's interior. The irony of his situation wasn't lost on him. Here he was, a former businessman, now diving headfirst into the world of counterfeit money.

As he approached a red light, Tom's mind wandered to Sofia. "She's sharp, that one," he mused. "Can't let my guard down for a second."

The light turned green, and Tom accelerated, his car purring smoothly as it picked up speed. He felt a familiar tingle of anticipation in his gut, reminiscent of closing big deals in his factory days.

"It's just another transaction," he reassured himself. "Albeit with slightly higher stakes."

Tom's eyes flicked to the rearview mirror, a habit he'd developed since embarking on this venture. The road behind him was clear, but he couldn't shake the feeling that he was being watched.

"Paranoia," he scoffed. "Get a grip, Beauchamp. You're not in a spy movie."

As he turned onto his street, Tom's excitement began to give way to the weight of reality. The risks he was taking, the potential consequences – they all came crashing down on him at once.

"What have I gotten myself into?" he whispered, his voice barely audible over the engine's purr.

But even as doubt crept in, Tom felt a surge of determination. He'd come too far to back out now. Whatever challenges lay ahead, he'd face them head-on.

"Time to put that meticulous planning to good use," he said, pulling into his driveway. "Let's see if this old dog can learn some new tricks."

Chapter 9

Tom Beauchamp sat at his polished mahogany desk, fingers hovering over the keyboard as he prepared to dive into the murky waters of the dark web. The soft glow of the monitor illuminated his graying hair and the deep lines etched around his eyes—evidence of years spent hunched over spreadsheets and factory blueprints.

He took a deep breath, steadying his nerves. "Alright, Tom," he muttered to himself, "time to put on your game face."

With practiced keystrokes, he navigated through encrypted channels and anonymous forums. The familiar rush of adrenaline coursed through his veins as he crafted his first message to a potential buyer.

"Greetings, esteemed colleague," Tom typed, his fingers dancing across the keys. "I trust this message finds you well. I'm reaching out to offer a unique opportunity—premium quality notes at an unbeatable price. Discretion assured."

He hit send, then leaned back in his chair, running a hand through his hair. The waiting game had begun.

To Tom's surprise, a response pinged back almost immediately. His heart raced as he opened the message.

"Interesting proposition," the reply read. "What makes your product stand out?"

Tom allowed himself a small smile. This was his moment to shine.

"Quality, my friend," he typed back. "Each note is a work of art, indistinguishable from the real thing. And at 60% of face value, you won't find a better deal anywhere."

The buyer seemed intrigued, and soon Tom found himself deep in negotiations. His confidence grew with each exchange, his natural charm translating surprisingly well to the digital realm.

Just as Tom thought he had the deal in the bag, a new message popped up that made his stomach drop.

"How do I know these aren't just photocopies? Prove they're the real deal."

Tom's mind raced. He hadn't prepared for this level of scrutiny so soon. Sweat beaded on his forehead as he frantically searched for a response that wouldn't give away his inexperience.

"Well," he typed, trying to inject a lighthearted tone into his words, "I could tell you they're so real, even George Washington does a double-take when he sees them. But I understand your caution. How about we start with a small sample order?"

As soon as he hit send, Tom winced. Too jokey? Too desperate? He held his breath, waiting for the response.

The silence stretched on, each second feeling like an eternity. Tom's leg bounced nervously under the desk, his earlier confidence evaporating like morning dew.

Finally, a reply came through. "Your humor doesn't inspire confidence. I need concrete proof, not jokes."

Tom's heart sank. He'd overplayed his hand, and now the whole deal was slipping away. He stared at the screen, mind blank, as he tried to salvage the situation.

"Come on, think," he urged himself. "There's got to be a way out of this mess."

Tom's eyes darted around his home office, landing on a framed dollar bill he'd kept as a memento from his first paycheck. Inspiration struck. He leaned forward, fingers flying across the keyboard.

"You're right, and I apologize. Let me demonstrate my expertise. Did you know the dollar bill has a hidden security thread that glows red under UV light? It's embedded vertically in the paper, visible from both sides. I can provide a sample that passes this test."

Tom held his breath, hoping his knowledge would impress the skeptical buyer. After a moment, a reply pinged.

"Interesting. What about the color-shifting ink?"

A small smile tugged at Tom's lips. He was on familiar ground now.

"Absolutely. The number '10' on a $10 bill shifts from copper to green when tilted. It's a feature I'm particularly proud of replicating."

The conversation continued, Tom detailing intricate security features with growing confidence. His years of meticulous research were paying off.

"Very well," the buyer finally conceded. "You've piqued my interest. Let's proceed with a small order."

Tom exhaled in relief, his shoulders relaxing. He'd dodged a bullet.

Just as he was about to finalize the details, a new message popped up from an unfamiliar username: "CryptoKing99."

"Heard you're the man with the magic paper. I want in, but I've got some... unique requests."

Tom furrowed his brow, curiosity piqued. "I'm listening. What did you have in mind?"

"First off, I want my bills to smell like bubblegum. Non-negotiable."

Tom blinked, wondering if he'd read that correctly. "I'm sorry, you want them to smell like... bubblegum?"

"That's right, Tommyboy. And I want a tiny hologram of Nicolas Cage hidden in the corner. Oh, and they need to be waterproof. I've had some... incidents."

Tom pinched the bridge of his nose, stifling a laugh. This was either a joke or the most eccentric buyer he'd ever encountered. Either way, he needed to tread carefully.

"Well, CryptoKing99," Tom typed, choosing his words carefully, "you certainly have a flair for the unique. While I appreciate your creativity, I'm afraid some of those features might draw unwanted attention."

Tom's fingers hovered over the keyboard, his mind racing to find a diplomatic response. He was about to type when a sharp knock at the door made him jump.

"Police! Open up!" a gruff voice called from the other side.

Tom's heart leapt into his throat. He quickly closed his laptop, his palms sweating as he scanned the room for any incriminating evidence. "Just a moment!" he called out, trying to keep his voice steady. He grabbed a stack of papers from his desk, shoving them into a hidden compartment behind a loose floorboard.

Taking a deep breath, Tom opened the door with what he hoped was a casual smile. "Good evening, officers. How can I help you?"

Two stern-faced policemen stood in the hallway. "We've had reports of suspicious activity in this building. Mind if we take a look around?"

Tom's mind raced. "Of course not," he said, stepping aside. "Though I'm not sure what you're looking for. I'm just a boring businessman working from home these days."

As the officers began their search, Tom's eyes darted nervously around the room. He noticed a stray counterfeit bill peeking out from under a magazine on the coffee table.

"So, what kind of business are you in, Mr...?" one officer asked.

"Beauchamp. Tom Beauchamp," he replied, inching towards the coffee table. "I'm in... um... financial consulting."

Tom casually picked up the magazine, deftly sliding the hidden bill into his pocket. "Coffee, gentlemen? I was just about to make a fresh pot."

The officers declined, continuing their search. Tom's heart pounded as they neared his laptop, but they moved past it without a second glance.

After what felt like an eternity, the police concluded their search. "Everything seems to be in order, Mr. Beauchamp. Sorry for the disturbance."

As Tom closed the door behind them, he leaned against it, exhaling deeply. That was too close. But as the adrenaline subsided, a grin spread across his face. He'd pulled it off. Maybe he was better at this than he thought.

Tom's moment of relief was short-lived. As he turned away from the door, his phone buzzed with a text from an unknown number:

"Nice work with the cops, Beauchamp. But you're playing in my sandbox now. Coffee tomorrow, 10 AM, Grind & Shine. Don't be late."

Tom frowned, his mind racing. Who could have sent this? He peered out the window, scanning the street below, but saw nothing suspicious.

"Damn it," he muttered, running a hand through his graying hair. "Just what I need. A rival."

The next morning, Tom arrived at Grind & Shine five minutes early, his nerves on edge. He ordered a latte and chose a table with a clear view of the entrance. At precisely 10 AM, a man in a tailored suit sauntered in, his eyes locking onto Tom immediately.

"Ah, the infamous Tom Beauchamp," the man said, sliding into the seat across from him. "I'm Jack. Let's chat about your little... side business."

Tom's jaw clenched. "I'm afraid I don't know what you're talking about," he replied, his tone measured.

Jack laughed, a harsh sound that grated on Tom's nerves. "Oh, come on. We're both in the same game. But there's only room for one counterfeiter in this town, and I was here first."

Before Tom could respond, he noticed two police officers entering the café. His heart rate spiked.

"Well, well," Jack smirked. "Looks like you've got company. How will you talk your way out of this one, Tom?"

Tom's mind raced, his eyes darting between Jack and the approaching officers. He needed an escape plan, and fast.

Tom's heart pounded as he stared at the stack of counterfeit bills on his kitchen table. A single bead of sweat trickled down his temple as he scrutinized each note under a magnifying glass.

"Damn it," he muttered, his fingers tracing the slightly misaligned watermark. "How did I miss this?"

The phone rang, startling him. Tom fumbled for it, recognizing the number of his most recent buyer.

"Hello, Mr. Johnson," Tom answered, his voice steady despite his racing pulse.

"Beauchamp, we have a problem," Johnson growled. "These bills... they're not up to your usual standard."

Tom swallowed hard, his mind already formulating a plan. "I assure you, Mr. Johnson, I take quality very seriously. I'll personally review every bill and replace any that don't meet our agreed-upon specifications."

"You'd better," Johnson warned. "I have a big transaction coming up, and I can't afford any slip-ups."

After hanging up, Tom rubbed his temples. "Okay, think," he murmured to himself. "I can fix this. I have to fix this."

He spent the next 48 hours hunched over his printing equipment, meticulously adjusting settings and recalibrating machines. Sleep became a luxury he couldn't afford.

As dawn broke on the third day, Tom held up a freshly printed bill, a triumphant smile spreading across his weary face. "Perfect," he whispered.

Later that afternoon, Tom waited nervously at a bustling café, a briefcase of corrected bills by his feet. A man in a navy suit approached, looking around suspiciously.

"Mr. Johnson?" Tom inquired, standing to greet him.

The man's brow furrowed. "No, I'm looking for a Tom Beauchamp. Are you him?"

Tom froze, his mind racing. This wasn't Johnson. "I... uh, yes, that's me," he stammered, trying to maintain his composure.

The man grinned, extending his hand. "Great! I'm Bob, your new buyer. Ready to do business?"

Tom's eyes widened as he realized the mix-up. He glanced around frantically, spotting another man eyeing them from across the café. That must be Johnson.

"Of course, Bob," Tom said smoothly, his quick thinking kicking in. "Why don't we step outside for a moment? I have something to show you."

As they walked out, Tom's mind whirled. How was he going to juggle two transactions without arousing suspicion? He chuckled inwardly at the absurdity of it all. Just another day in the life of Tom Beauchamp, accidental counterfeiter extraordinaire.

Tom's heart raced as he fumbled with his coffee cup, nearly spilling it on the pristine white tablecloth. Across from him sat Sarah Jennings, a sharp-eyed journalist with a notepad and a relentless curiosity.

"So, Mr. Beauchamp," Sarah began, her pen poised, "I've been hearing whispers about a sudden influx of high-quality counterfeit bills in the area. As a respected local businessman, have you noticed anything... unusual?"

Tom forced a casual laugh, though it came out more like a nervous hiccup. "Counterfeit bills? That's quite a story, Ms. Jennings. But I'm afraid my expertise lies more in brake pads than banking."

Sarah leaned forward, her eyes gleaming. "Interesting you should mention brake pads. I've been looking into your recent sale of your factory. Quite a windfall, wasn't it?"

Tom's mind raced. How much did she know? He took a sip of coffee to buy time, scalding his tongue in the process. "Well," he said, wincing slightly, "I'd hardly call it a windfall. Just fair compensation for years of hard work."

As Tom fumbled for a way to steer the conversation away from dangerous waters, his phone buzzed. He glanced down, his blood running cold as he read the message:

"Face-to-face meeting. Tomorrow. No excuses. - The Shark"

Tom's hands trembled as he set the phone down. The Shark was notorious in the underground currency world - ruthless, paranoid, and not someone to be trifled with.

"Everything alright?" Sarah asked, her journalist's instinct picking up on his sudden discomfort.

"Fine, fine," Tom said, forcing a smile. "Just a... business matter that needs attention."

As he looked at Sarah's probing gaze and thought of the looming meeting with The Shark, Tom felt the walls closing in. How had his carefully laid plans spiraled so quickly out of control?

Tom's heart raced as he paced his hotel room, his normally meticulous appearance disheveled. He ran a hand through his graying hair, muttering to himself, "Get it together, Tom. You've faced tougher challenges than this."

He paused at the window, staring out at the city lights. The Shark's message weighed heavily on his mind. A face-to-face meeting. It went against everything he'd planned, every precaution he'd taken.

His phone buzzed again. Tom flinched, expecting another ominous message. Instead, it was a text from his daughter: "Good luck on your business trip, Dad! Knock 'em dead!"

Tom's throat tightened. If she only knew.

He turned from the window and began meticulously laying out his suit for tomorrow's meeting. Each crease perfectly aligned, each button securely fastened. It was a ritual that usually calmed him, but tonight it felt like preparing for his own funeral.

"What if it's a trap?" he wondered aloud, his voice echoing in the empty room. "What if The Shark is working with the authorities?"

Tom shook his head, trying to dispel the paranoid thoughts. He needed to focus, to prepare. He opened his briefcase, double-checking the samples he'd bring to the meeting. His fingers traced the intricate designs of the counterfeit bills, marveling at their authenticity.

"It's just another transaction," he told himself, not quite believing it. "Just like selling brake pads, only... with slightly higher stakes."

As he closed the briefcase, his hand lingered on the cool metal. Tomorrow would determine everything - his future, his freedom, the success of his audacious plan. With a deep breath, Tom switched off the light, plunging the room into darkness.

Sleep, however, remained elusive. As he lay in bed, staring at the ceiling, Tom couldn't shake the feeling that he was walking into the lion's den. What awaited him at tomorrow's meeting? And more importantly, would he be able to walk away from it?

Chapter 10

Tom's footsteps echoed through the dimly lit warehouse as he paced back and forth, the rhythmic thud of his shoes on concrete punctuated by the occasional creak of aging machinery. His makeshift printing facility, nestled in the heart of an abandoned industrial complex, had always felt like a sanctuary. Today, it felt more like a cage.

He paused mid-stride, his eyes darting to a shadowy corner. Was that movement? Just a trick of the light, he assured himself, running a hand through his graying hair. Still, he couldn't shake the feeling that something was... off.

"Get it together, Tom," he muttered, his voice barely above a whisper. "You're just being paranoid."

But was he? The nagging doubt gnawed at him as he resumed his pacing, each step measured and deliberate. He'd spent years planning this operation, meticulously crafting every detail. It was his ticket out of the mundane life he'd left behind, a chance at the comfort and security he'd always dreamed of. And yet, here he was, jumping at shadows.

Tom's gaze swept across the room, taking in the familiar sight of printing presses and stacks of paper. Everything was in its place, just as he'd left it. So why did it all feel so... wrong?

"You're losing it, old man," he chuckled nervously, the sound echoing off the bare walls. "Next thing you know, you'll be seeing undercover agents lurking in every corner."

Little did Tom know, his offhand comment wasn't far from the truth. Across the street, in a nondescript van parked among the derelict buildings, Marc-André Leblanc sat hunched over a bank of monitors. His piercing blue eyes were fixed on the grainy black-and-white image of Tom's anxious pacing.

"Got you, my friend," Marc-André murmured, a hint of satisfaction in his voice. He'd spent months infiltrating the local criminal underworld, slowly working his way closer to Tom's operation. Now, he was tantalizingly close to bringing it all crashing down.

Marc-André leaned back in his chair, stretching his athletic frame. He'd been in this van for hours, but his focus never wavered. That's what made him one of the best in the business - his relentless determination and unwavering patience.

"Just a little longer," he told himself, his tone measured and calm despite the tension of the situation. "Let's see what you're up to, Mr. Beauchamp."

Back in the warehouse, Tom had finally stopped pacing. He stood in front of one of the printing presses, his fingers tracing the cool metal surface. It was almost soothing, a tangible reminder of everything he'd built.

"This is your ticket to a better life," he reminded himself, his voice carrying the weight of years of hard work and missed opportunities. "Don't let your nerves ruin everything now."

With a deep breath, Tom squared his shoulders and turned back to his work. He had orders to fill, after all. And if there really was something to worry about... well, he'd cross that bridge when he came to it.

As Tom busied himself with the printing press, Marc-André allowed himself a small smile. The pieces were falling into place. It was only a matter of time now.

Tom's fingers trembled slightly as he adjusted the printing press, his eyes darting to the warehouse door every few seconds. Something felt off about his latest interaction with his regular buyers. The way they'd hesitated before accepting the shipment, their forced smiles, the whispered conversation he'd overheard...

"Get a grip, Tom," he muttered to himself, wiping sweat from his brow. "You're just being paranoid."

But the nagging feeling wouldn't subside. He replayed the meeting in his mind, analyzing every word, every gesture. Had Johnson always fidgeted that much? And why did Martinez keep glancing at his watch?

Tom's internal spiral was interrupted by the shrill ring of his burner phone. He froze, staring at the device as if it might bite him. Taking a deep breath, he answered.

"Hello?" he said, trying to keep his voice steady.

"Mr. Beauchamp," a distorted voice crackled through the speaker. "I hope I'm not interrupting anything... important."

Tom's heart raced. "Who is this?"

"Let's just say I'm an interested party," the voice continued. "One who knows about your little side business. The question is, what are we going to do about it?"

Tom's mouth went dry. "I don't know what you're talking about," he managed, his mind racing through possible escape routes.

A low chuckle came through the line. "Oh, I think you do. We'll be in touch, Tom. Sweet dreams."

The line went dead, leaving Tom standing in stunned silence, the weight of his choices pressing down on him like never before.

Tom slumped into his chair, his mind a whirlwind of conflicting thoughts. He ran his fingers through his graying hair, his eyes fixed on the printing press that had become both his salvation and his potential downfall.

"What have I gotten myself into?" he whispered, the weight of his decisions pressing down on him like a physical force.

The sound of the door opening startled him. Giselle walked in, her red hair catching the dim light. She took one look at Tom's face and frowned.

"Tom? What's wrong?" she asked, her voice tinged with concern.

He sighed heavily. "I don't know, Giselle. I just... I can't shake this feeling that we're in over our heads."

Giselle pulled up a chair next to him, her green eyes searching his face. "Is this about the new buyers? I've been meaning to talk to you about them."

Tom leaned back, forcing a smile. "Oh? And what pearls of wisdom does my beautiful partner have for me today?"

"I'm serious, Tom," Giselle said, her tone firm. "Something feels off about them. The way they look at us, like they're studying us. I think we should be careful."

Tom waved his hand dismissively. "You're overthinking it, chérie. They're just new, that's all. They'll settle in."

Giselle's brow furrowed. "But what if they're not who they say they are? What if—"

"What if the sky falls tomorrow?" Tom interrupted, his voice taking on an edge. "We can't live our lives in fear, Giselle. I've worked too hard to back out now."

"I'm not saying we should back out," Giselle replied, her accent becoming more pronounced as her frustration grew. "I'm saying we should be cautious. Use that meticulous brain of yours to consider all possibilities."

Tom stood up, pacing the small room. His mind raced, weighing the risks against the potential rewards. The thought of losing everything he'd built, of disappointing Giselle, of ending up behind bars – it all swirled in his head like a tempest.

"I can handle this," he said, more to himself than to Giselle. "I've come too far to turn back now. We just need to be smarter, more careful."

Giselle stood, placing a hand on his arm. "Tom, please. Just listen to me for once. Something's not right, and I think we need to—"

"Enough!" Tom snapped, immediately regretting his tone as he saw the hurt flash across Giselle's face. He softened his voice. "I'm sorry, chérie. I just... I need you to trust me on this. I can outsmart them, whoever they are. We've come too far to give up now."

Giselle's shoulders sagged slightly, but she nodded. "Okay, Tom. I trust you. Just... be careful, please?"

As Tom pulled her into a hug, he couldn't shake the nagging feeling that maybe, just maybe, he was making the biggest mistake of his life.

Tom wiped the sweat from his brow as he adjusted the printing press, the familiar hum of machinery filling the air. The door creaked open, and he tensed, relaxing only when he saw the friendly face of Marc, the new regular at his local café.

"Hey there, Tom," Marc called out, his voice warm and inviting. "Thought I'd drop by and see your setup. Impressive stuff!"

Tom's eyes darted around the room, his heart racing. "Marc, right? How did you find this place?"

Marc chuckled, his blue eyes twinkling. "You mentioned it the other day over coffee. Hope you don't mind the surprise visit."

Tom forced a smile, his mind whirring. Had he really let that slip? "Not at all. Just finishing up some work."

As they chatted, Tom couldn't shake the feeling that Marc's gaze lingered a bit too long on the stacks of paper and machinery. He found himself sharing more than he intended, Marc's easy-going nature drawing him in.

"So, what exactly do you print here?" Marc asked casually, running a hand along a nearby shelf.

Tom hesitated, his inner voice screaming caution. "Oh, you know, just standard business materials. Nothing too exciting."

Marc nodded, his expression unreadable. "Right, right. Well, it's fascinating stuff, Tom. We should grab coffee again soon."

As Marc left, Tom's eyes caught a glint of something in the corner. His blood ran cold as he approached, discovering a tiny camera hidden behind a stack of papers.

"Merde," he whispered, his hands shaking as he plucked the device from its hiding spot. How long had it been there? Who placed it? His mind raced through possibilities, each more terrifying than the last.

Tom slumped into a nearby chair, the weight of his choices crushing down on him. He'd always prided himself on being three steps ahead, but now he felt like he was fumbling in the dark. As he stared at the camera in his palm, one thought echoed in his mind: "What have I gotten myself into?"

Tom's heart raced as he scanned the room, his eyes darting from corner to corner. "Gotta clean house," he muttered, his voice barely above a whisper. He grabbed a trash bag and began shoving stacks of counterfeit bills into it, his movements frantic yet purposeful.

As he worked, Tom's mind whirled. "Just act normal," he reminded himself, forcing a smile as he waved to his neighbor through the window. The neighbor waved back, oblivious to the panic behind Tom's facade.

Tom's phone buzzed. It was Jacques, one of his regular buyers. He stared at the screen, his finger hovering over the answer button. After a moment's hesitation, he declined the call.

"Sorry, Jacques," Tom murmured, deleting the contact. "Can't risk it."

He moved to his computer, fingers flying across the keyboard as he erased files and cleared his browsing history. The sound of sirens in the distance made him jump, his nerves frayed to the breaking point.

"Get it together, Tom," he chastised himself, taking a deep breath. He glanced at his watch. "Still time for my usual coffee run. Keep up appearances."

As he locked up, Tom nodded curtly to the barista who greeted him by name. "Just a small black coffee today, Marie," he said, his usual warmth noticeably absent.

Marie tilted her head, concern etching her features. "Everything okay, Tom? You seem... off."

Tom forced a chuckle, though it sounded hollow even to his own ears. "Just a bit under the weather. Nothing to worry about."

As he left the cafe, Tom couldn't shake the feeling that every pair of eyes was on him, judging, knowing. He quickened his pace, eager to return to the relative safety of his printing facility.

"You're just being paranoid," he told himself, but the words rang false. In this game, paranoia might be the only thing keeping him one step ahead of disaster.

Tom's eyes darted nervously around the cozy café as he approached the counter, his mind still racing from the events of the past few days. The rich aroma of freshly ground coffee beans did little to soothe his frayed nerves.

"The usual, please," he mumbled to the barista, fishing for his wallet.

As he turned to find a seat, he collided head-on with another patron, sending both their coffees flying.

"Oh, for crying out—" Tom began, then froze. The man he'd bumped into was none other than Marc-André Leblanc, the new face in his circle of buyers.

Marc-André's eyebrows shot up in recognition, but he quickly schooled his features. "My apologies, sir," he said smoothly, grabbing napkins to mop up the spill.

Tom's heart hammered in his chest. "No, no, it was my fault," he replied, forcing a laugh. "Clumsy me."

They locked eyes for a moment, a silent acknowledgment passing between them. Tom wondered if his panic was as obvious as it felt.

"Let me buy you another coffee," Marc-André offered, his tone casual but his gaze intense.

"That's really not necessary," Tom insisted, backing away. "I should be going anyway."

As he hurried out of the café, Tom's mind raced. What were the odds of running into Marc-André here? Was it truly a coincidence?

Later that evening, Tom paced his printing facility, replaying the café encounter in his mind. The sound of the door opening made him jump.

"You're late," he snapped at the entering figure, one of his regular buyers.

The man, a burly fellow named Carl, looked taken aback. "Traffic was hell. What's got you so wound up?"

Tom's eyes narrowed. "You tell me, Carl. Or should I even call you that?"

Carl's confusion was evident. "What are you talking about, Tom?"

"Don't play dumb," Tom hissed, advancing on Carl. "You're working with them, aren't you? The cops?"

Carl raised his hands defensively. "Whoa, man. You're not making any sense. I'm just here for the usual pickup."

Tom's paranoia battled with his rational mind. Could he trust Carl? Or was this all part of an elaborate sting?

"Prove it," Tom demanded, his voice shaking. "Prove you're not an undercover agent."

Carl's face cycled through bewilderment, anger, and finally, pity. "Tom, buddy, I think you need to take a breather. This stress is getting to you."

As Carl's words sank in, Tom felt a wave of shame wash over him. What was he doing? He was alienating one of his most reliable contacts based on nothing but suspicion.

"I... I'm sorry, Carl," Tom stammered, running a hand through his graying hair. "You're right. I haven't been myself lately."

Carl nodded cautiously. "Maybe you should consider taking a break, Tom. This business... it can mess with your head."

Tom sank into a nearby chair, suddenly feeling every one of his years. "Yeah," he murmured, "maybe you're right."

Tom's gaze drifted to the window, watching passersby on the street below. Each face seemed to hide secrets, every glance potentially hostile. He sighed heavily, his shoulders slumping.

"I don't know who to trust anymore, Carl," Tom confessed, his voice barely above a whisper. "Every shadow looks like a threat. Every phone call could be the one that brings it all crashing down."

Carl shifted uncomfortably. "Look, Tom, I—"

"No, it's okay," Tom interrupted, holding up a hand. "You don't need to say anything. I think... I think I need to step back for a bit."

He stood up, pacing the room with measured steps. "I've worked too hard to lose it all now. But if I keep going like this, I'm going to make a mistake. A big one."

Tom's mind raced, weighing options and risks. Finally, he turned to Carl, his expression resolute.

"I'm shutting down the operation. Temporarily," he said, his tone leaving no room for argument. "Just until I can figure out what's really going on."

Carl's eyebrows shot up. "Are you sure that's wise? Your buyers—"

"My buyers will have to wait," Tom cut in firmly. "Right now, I need to focus on protecting myself and finding out who's been sniffing around my business."

He walked over to his desk, pulling out a notepad. "I'm going to need your help, Carl. I want you to keep your ear to the ground, see if you can pick up any chatter about new players or increased police activity."

Carl nodded slowly. "Alright, Tom. If that's what you think is best. But what about your stock?"

Tom's lips quirked into a humorless smile. "Already got a plan for that. It's amazing how quickly you can clear out a warehouse when you need to."

As he jotted down notes, Tom felt a strange mix of fear and exhilaration. He was taking a risk, but it felt good to be doing something proactive.

"We'll weather this storm, Carl," he said, more to himself than his companion. "And when we come out the other side, we'll be stronger for it."

But even as he spoke the words, a nagging doubt lingered in the back of his mind. Could he really outsmart whoever was after him? Or was he just delaying the inevitable?

Tom's pen hovered over the notepad, his brow furrowed in concentration. The quiet hum of the air conditioning seemed to amplify the tension in the room. He looked up at Carl, his eyes glinting with a mix of determination and uncertainty.

"There's one more thing," Tom said, his voice low and measured. "I need you to set up a meeting with our friend in customs. It's time we called in that favor."

Carl's eyebrows shot up. "Are you sure about that, Tom? Once we involve him, there's no going back."

Tom leaned back in his chair, running a hand through his graying hair. "I know the risks, but we're past the point of playing it safe. This could be our ace in the hole."

As he spoke, Tom's gaze drifted to the window. The city lights twinkled in the distance, a stark contrast to the shadows that seemed to be closing in around him. He couldn't shake the feeling that someone was watching, waiting for him to make a mistake.

"What if it's not enough?" Carl asked, breaking into Tom's thoughts. "What if they're already one step ahead?"

Tom turned back to face him, a wry smile playing on his lips. "Then we'll just have to be two steps ahead, won't we?" He paused, his expression growing serious. "But you're right to be cautious. We can't afford any slip-ups now."

He stood up, pacing the room as he often did when deep in thought. "Here's what we're going to do," Tom began, his voice taking on the authoritative tone he'd used so often in his days running the brake pad factory. "First, we'll..."

Suddenly, a sharp knock at the door cut him off mid-sentence. Tom froze, his heart pounding in his chest. He exchanged a quick, panicked glance with Carl before calling out, his voice remarkably steady, "Who is it?"

The answer that came through the door sent a chill down Tom's spine, leaving him wondering if his carefully laid plans were about to come crashing down around him.

Chapter 11

Giselle's fingers danced across the keyboard, her emerald eyes scanning the screen as she browsed through Tom's emails. The soft glow of the monitor illuminated her face in the dimly lit study, casting shadows that accentuated her furrowed brow.

"Just a quick peek," she murmured to herself, justifying her intrusion. "What Tom doesn't know won't hurt him."

As she scrolled, a peculiar email caught her attention. The subject line read: "Re: Transaction Details - Urgent." Giselle's curiosity piqued, she clicked it open, her heart quickening as she read the contents.

"Well, well, well," she whispered, leaning closer to the screen. "What do we have here?"

The email was vague, but something about the tone and the few details provided set off alarm bells in Giselle's mind. She bit her lower lip, a habit she'd developed whenever deep in thought.

"I've got a bad feeling about this," she muttered, reaching for her phone. "Time to do some digging."

With nimble fingers, Giselle began cross-referencing the email address with her list of law enforcement contacts. She'd accumulated quite a network over the years, a byproduct of her insatiable curiosity and Tom's... unconventional business practices.

As she worked, Giselle couldn't help but chuckle at the absurdity of her situation. "Here I am, playing detective while Tom's probably dreaming about his next big score. Oh, the things we do for love."

Suddenly, her phone pinged. Giselle's eyes widened as she read the message, her breath catching in her throat.

"No way," she gasped, double-checking the information. "It can't be."

But there it was, clear as day. The email address was linked to an undercover agent named Marc-André Leblanc. Giselle's mind raced, piecing together the implications of this discovery.

"Oh, Tom," she sighed, running a hand through her fiery red hair. "What have you gotten us into this time?"

Giselle leaned back in her chair, the weight of her discovery settling on her shoulders. She knew she had to tell Tom, but how? And more importantly, what would they do next?

"Well," she said to the empty room, a wry smile playing on her lips, "looks like our little counterfeit operation just got a whole lot more interesting."

Giselle's fingers flew across the keyboard, her green eyes narrowed in concentration as she delved deeper into Marc-André Leblanc's background. The more she uncovered, the more her stomach twisted with a mix of fascination and dread.

"Mon Dieu," she muttered, scrolling through news articles and police reports. "This guy's like a dog with a bone."

Marc-André's name appeared in connection with several high-profile cases, each more impressive than the last. Drug busts, money laundering operations, even an international art theft ring. In every instance, Marc-André had been relentless, pursuing leads until he brought down his targets.

Giselle chewed her lower lip, her mind racing. "Tom needs to know about this," she said to herself, then paused. "But how can I tell him without revealing I've been snooping?"

As if on cue, she heard Tom's heavy footsteps approaching. Quickly, she minimized her browser windows and swiveled in her chair, plastering on a smile as he entered the room.

"Hey there, handsome," she said, her voice only slightly strained. "How's the grand plan coming along?"

Tom's eyes lit up, that familiar spark of ambition shining through his weariness. "It's all falling into place, Giselle. I've got a meeting set up with the buyers next week. If all goes well, we'll be sitting pretty in no time."

Giselle's heart sank. She wanted to shake him, to make him see the danger they were in. Instead, she asked, "Are you sure about these buyers, Tom? We don't know much about them."

Tom waved off her concern. "I've vetted them thoroughly. Trust me, everything's under control."

As he rambled on about exchange rates and offshore accounts, Giselle's mind whirled. How could she protect Tom from himself without betraying his trust? The irony wasn't lost on her – here she was, worrying about trust while keeping secrets of her own.

"You're awfully quiet," Tom said, interrupting her thoughts. "Everything okay?"

Giselle forced a laugh. "Just tired, I guess. All this cloak-and-dagger stuff is exhausting."

Tom's face softened. He crossed the room and planted a kiss on her forehead. "It'll all be worth it in the end, you'll see. Now, how about some dinner? I'm thinking takeout tonight."

As Tom left to order food, Giselle turned back to her computer, her resolve strengthening. She had to find a way to protect them both, even if Tom was too blinded by ambition to see the danger.

"Alright, Marc-André Leblanc," she whispered, reopening her research. "Let's see what other skeletons you've got hiding in your closet."

Giselle's fingers flew across the keyboard as she dug deeper into Marc-André Leblanc's habits. A smile tugged at her lips when she stumbled upon a promising lead.

"Bingo," she murmured, scribbling an address on a scrap of paper.

The next morning, Giselle found herself perched on a bench across from Le Petit Café, a quaint coffee shop nestled in a bustling downtown street. She sipped her latte, eyes scanning the crowd over the rim of her sunglasses.

"Come on, Marc-André," she whispered. "Don't let me down now."

A businessman hurried past, nearly knocking over her carefully positioned shopping bags. Giselle readjusted them, ensuring they still provided adequate cover.

Just as she was beginning to doubt her intel, a man matching Marc-André's description approached the café. Giselle's pulse quickened.

"Mon Dieu," she breathed. "It's really him."

The man paused at the entrance, checking his watch. Giselle leaned forward, straining to catch every detail. He was tall, with salt-and-pepper hair and a neatly trimmed beard. His posture screamed law enforcement, even in casual clothes.

As he reached for the door handle, Giselle's phone buzzed. Tom's name flashed on the screen.

"Merde," she muttered, silencing the call. "Not now, Tom."

She looked up just in time to see Marc-André disappear into the café. Giselle's mind raced. Should she follow him inside? The risk of being recognized was high, but the potential payoff...

"Oh, what the hell," she said, gathering her things. "In for a penny, in for a pound."

Giselle's heart pounded as she trailed Marc-André out of the café, her footsteps light and measured. The scent of coffee lingered in the air, mingling with the crisp autumn breeze. She kept her distance, weaving through the crowd with practiced ease.

"Just act natural," she reminded herself, adjusting her scarf. "You're just another face in the crowd."

Marc-André turned abruptly, ducking into a narrow alley. Giselle hesitated, then followed, pressing herself against the cool brick wall. She peered around the corner, her breath catching as she spotted Marc-André meeting with another man.

"This is it," she thought, fumbling for her smartphone. Her fingers trembled slightly as she opened the camera app, switching it to video mode.

The two men spoke in hushed tones, their words barely audible over the distant hum of traffic. Giselle inched closer, straining to hear.

"...counterfeits flooding the market," Marc-André was saying. "We're close to pinpointing the source."

The other man nodded. "And the Beauchamp lead?"

Giselle's stomach dropped. She zoomed in, desperate to catch every word.

Marc-André smirked. "Let's just say Mr. Beauchamp should watch his step. We're closing in."

"Oh, Tom," Giselle thought, her mind racing. "What have you gotten us into?"

She fought the urge to flee, knowing this information was too valuable to miss. As the men continued their clandestine chat, Giselle recorded every damning detail, her green eyes wide with a mix of fear and determination.

"We'll make our move soon," Marc-André concluded. "Be ready."

As the meeting wrapped up, Giselle quickly pocketed her phone and melted back into the bustling street, her heart hammering in her chest. She hailed a taxi, her mind swirling with the implications of what she'd just witnessed.

"Where to, miss?" the driver asked.

Giselle hesitated, then gave Tom's address. "Time to face the music," she murmured, bracing herself for the difficult conversation ahead.

Giselle burst through the front door, her fiery red hair disheveled from the wind. Tom looked up from his laptop, his graying eyebrows furrowing at her flustered appearance.

"Tom, we need to talk," Giselle said, her voice tight with urgency. She pulled out her smartphone, her hands shaking slightly. "I've found something, and it's not good."

Tom's tired eyes narrowed. "What's going on, Giselle? You look like you've seen a ghost."

Giselle took a deep breath, her green eyes locking onto Tom's. "It's about the buyers. They're not who we think they are."

She played the recording, watching Tom's face carefully. His expression shifted from confusion to disbelief as Marc-André's words filled the room.

"This can't be right," Tom said, shaking his head. "Our operation is airtight. We've planned for every contingency."

Giselle placed a hand on his arm. "Tom, please. Listen to me. This is serious. They mentioned you by name."

Tom stood up, pacing the room. "It's probably just a coincidence. There are plenty of Beauchamps in Quebec."

"But what if it's not?" Giselle pressed, her accent thickening with emotion. "We can't ignore this, Tom. We're in over our heads."

Tom ran a hand through his hair, his mind racing. "Let me hear it again," he said, reaching for the phone.

As the recording played once more, doubt began to creep into Tom's eyes. He sank back into his chair, the weight of realization settling on his shoulders.

"Mon Dieu," he whispered. "Could there be a mole?"

Giselle nodded grimly. "It's possible. We need to be careful, Tom. Very careful."

Tom's gaze drifted to the window, his ambitious dreams suddenly seeming very far away. "What have I gotten us into, Giselle?" he murmured, more to himself than to her.

The room fell silent, filled only with the heavy implications of their newfound knowledge and the uncertain future that lay ahead.

Tom's fingers drummed an anxious rhythm on the arm of his chair, his eyes darting between Giselle and the window. The sun was setting, casting long shadows across the room and painting the walls in hues of orange and red.

"We can't just give up now," Tom said, his voice tinged with frustration. "We've come too far, invested too much. There has to be a way around this."

Giselle let out an exasperated sigh, her green eyes flashing. "A way around law enforcement? Tom, be reasonable. This isn't like finding a loophole in tax laws."

"But think of the potential, Giselle!" Tom leaned forward, his voice rising with excitement. "If we can just get past this hurdle, we'll be set for life. No more worrying about retirement, about the future."

Giselle couldn't help but chuckle, despite the tension. "Oh, Tom. Your optimism is adorable, but misplaced. You sound like a kid planning to rob a candy store."

Tom's lips twitched, fighting a smile. "Well, at least I'd have good taste in targets."

Their laughter, brief and strained, filled the room before fading into a heavy silence.

"We can't ignore this, Tom," Giselle said softly, her hand finding his. "It's not just about the money anymore. It's about our safety."

Tom squeezed her hand, his resolve wavering. "I know, I know. But what do we do? We can't just walk away from everything we've built."

Giselle's eyes lit up with an idea. "Maybe we don't have to walk away entirely. What if we... pause? Take some time to gather more information about these buyers and their connection to the police?"

Tom mulled it over, his brow furrowed in concentration. "A temporary halt," he mused. "It could give us time to shore up our defenses, maybe even find a way to turn this to our advantage."

"Exactly," Giselle nodded, relief washing over her. "We proceed with caution, gather intel, and then decide our next move."

As the last rays of sunlight faded from the room, Tom and Giselle shared a look of determination, united in their decision to face the challenges ahead – together.

Giselle's fingers flew across the keyboard, her green eyes reflecting the glow of the computer screen. The soft tapping of keys filled the room as she dug deeper into the backgrounds of their potential buyers.

"Tom," she called out, her voice tinged with excitement. "I think I've found something interesting about one of the buyers."

Tom looked up from the stack of papers he was poring over, his graying hair disheveled. "What've you got, Giselle?"

She swiveled her chair to face him, a triumphant smile playing on her lips. "Remember Jacques Leblanc? Turns out he has a gambling problem. He's been frequenting underground casinos in Montreal."

Tom's eyebrows shot up. "Now that's something we can work with. Good job, chérie."

Giselle beamed, her curiosity piqued even further. "I'm going to keep digging. There might be more we can use."

As Giselle turned back to her research, Tom stood up and stretched, his joints popping. He walked over to the safe hidden behind a painting and carefully opened it.

"While you're playing detective," Tom said, his tone light but his eyes serious, "I'm going to upgrade our security. Can't be too careful with our little fortune here."

Giselle glanced over her shoulder, watching as Tom began meticulously organizing the counterfeit bills. "What do you have in mind?"

Tom held up a small device. "This beauty is a state-of-the-art motion sensor. I'm thinking of installing a few around the house."

"Motion sensors?" Giselle chuckled. "Tom Beauchamp, are we becoming paranoid?"

Tom grinned, but there was a hint of worry in his eyes. "Not paranoid, my dear. Just... cautious. Very, very cautious."

As they worked in comfortable silence, Giselle couldn't help but wonder how they'd ended up here - from a simple brake pad factory to this elaborate scheme. But looking at Tom's determined face, she knew there was no place she'd rather be.

Tom finished installing the last motion sensor and stepped back, admiring his handiwork. He turned to Giselle, who was still hunched over her laptop, her brow furrowed in concentration.

"Well, my dear," he said, his voice carrying a mix of pride and nervousness, "we're as fortified as Fort Knox now. How's your end coming along?"

Giselle looked up, her green eyes sparkling with excitement. "Tom, you won't believe what I've found. These buyers? They're not just connected to Marc-André. They have ties to a whole network of undercover agents across Quebec."

Tom's face paled slightly. "Mon Dieu," he whispered, running a hand through his graying hair. "This is bigger than we thought."

Giselle nodded, her red hair bouncing with the movement. "But here's the thing - they're not as united as they seem. I've uncovered some internal conflicts, power struggles. We might be able to use that to our advantage."

Tom sat down heavily next to her, his body tense but his mind racing. "You're right. If we play our cards right, we could turn them against each other."

Giselle placed a hand on his arm, her touch gentle but her voice firm. "It's risky, Tom. We're in deep already. Are you sure you want to push further?"

Tom looked at her, his eyes reflecting years of hard work and unfulfilled dreams. "What choice do we have, chérie? We've come too far to back out now."

Giselle nodded, a small smile playing on her lips. "Then we're in this together. To the end."

Tom chuckled, some of the tension leaving his shoulders. "To the end. God help us both."

As they sat there, surrounded by the fruits of their illicit labor and the weight of their decisions, Tom couldn't help but feel a strange mix of fear and exhilaration. Whatever came next, they'd face it side by side.

Chapter 12

The crisp autumn air nipped at Tom's face as he stepped out of his car, briefcase in hand. His eyes darted around the busy street, taking in the seemingly ordinary scene. But Tom knew better. He could feel the weight of unseen gazes upon him.

"Just another day at the office," Tom muttered to himself, straightening his tie with trembling fingers. He took a deep breath, willing his racing heart to slow. The familiar storefronts and bustling pedestrians blurred into the background as he focused on his target: the nondescript bank building across the street.

As Tom waited for the crosswalk signal, he caught a glimpse of movement in his peripheral vision. A man in a dark jacket leaned against a nearby lamppost, his eyes fixed on Tom. Another figure lurked in the shadows of an alleyway, speaking quietly into what appeared to be a radio.

Tom's palms grew sweaty around the handle of his briefcase. He knew what was inside - stacks of meticulously crafted counterfeit bills, the fruit of months of careful planning and sleepless nights. Now, it all seemed to be crumbling around him.

"Keep it together, Beauchamp," he whispered to himself as he crossed the street. "You've come too far to falter now."

As he approached the bank's entrance, Tom noticed a stocky man with salt-and-pepper hair standing near the door. The man's sharp eyes locked onto Tom, and a chill ran down his spine. He recognized Sergeant Jean-Guy Tremblay from his extensive research.

"Good morning, sir," Tremblay said, his voice gruff but not unfriendly. "Beautiful day for a stroll, isn't it?"

Tom forced a smile, hoping the tremor in his voice wasn't noticeable. "Indeed it is, officer. Just on my way to make a deposit."

Tremblay nodded, his piercing gaze never leaving Tom's face. "Of course. Don't let me keep you."

As Tom pushed open the heavy glass door, his mind raced. How had they found out? Where had he slipped up? He thought of Giselle waiting for him at home, her bright green eyes full of hope for their future. He couldn't let her down.

Inside the bank, Tom's eyes scanned for possible escape routes. The tellers behind their counters, the security guard by the door - were they all in on it? He felt like a rat in a maze, with Jean-Guy Tremblay and his team closing in from all sides.

"I can do this," Tom thought, gripping his briefcase tighter. "I just need to stay calm and think." But as he approached the teller's window, his heart pounding in his ears, Tom knew that his carefully constructed plan was unraveling faster than he could ever have imagined.

Tom's eyes darted around the bank, desperately searching for a way out, when suddenly a commotion erupted near the entrance. A flamboyantly dressed woman with a poodle tucked under her arm burst through the doors, her shrill voice echoing through the marble lobby.

"Fifi! Oh, Fifi! You naughty girl, come back here this instant!"

The tiny dog wriggled free and scampered across the polished floor, yapping excitedly. Tom watched in amazement as the woman's gaudy hat tumbled off, revealing a nest of shocking pink hair.

"This is my chance," Tom thought, his lips twitching with a mix of amusement and relief.

As bank patrons scrambled to avoid the careening canine, Tom edged towards the exit, trying to blend in with the chaos. He hunched his shoulders and affected a look of exasperation, muttering under his breath, "Well, I never..."

Just as freedom seemed within reach, a solid mass collided with Tom's side. He stumbled, nearly losing his grip on the briefcase, and found himself face-to-face with a young police officer.

"Oh, I'm so sorry, sir!" the officer exclaimed, steadying Tom with a hand on his arm.

Tom's heart leaped into his throat. "No harm done," he managed to croak out, praying the officer wouldn't recognize him.

The young man's eyes widened slightly, and Tom felt a bead of sweat trickle down his back. Had he given himself away?

Tom's mind raced as he searched for an escape route. The bustling crowd around him suddenly seemed like a lifeline. With a quick nod to the officer, he muttered, "Excuse me, I'm late for an appointment," and plunged into the sea of bodies.

His heart pounded in his ears as he weaved through the throng, acutely aware of the briefcase clutched tightly to his chest. The adrenaline surging through his veins made every sensation sharper - the brush of fabric against his arm, the cacophony of voices, the faint scent of perfume in the air.

"Just act natural," Tom coached himself silently. "You're just another face in the crowd."

He spotted a group of businessmen heading towards the exit and fell in step behind them, mimicking their purposeful stride. As they pushed through the revolving door, Tom allowed himself a small sigh of relief. The cool air outside hit his face, a stark contrast to the stuffy interior of the bank.

"I think I might actually pull this off," he thought, a glimmer of hope rising in his chest.

But fate had other plans. From behind him, a gruff voice cut through the noise of the street: "There he is! Don't let him get away!"

Tom's blood ran cold as he recognized the voice of Sergeant Jean-Guy Tremblay. He risked a glance over his shoulder and saw the determined face of the veteran officer, his eyes locked on Tom like a hawk eyeing its prey.

"Merde," Tom muttered, his carefully laid plans crumbling around him. He picked up his pace, ducking and weaving through the pedestrians on the sidewalk.

Sergeant Tremblay's voice boomed out again, "All units, suspect is heading east on Main Street. Cut him off at the intersection!"

Tom's mind raced, searching for options. "Think, Beauchamp, think!" he berated himself. "There's got to be a way out of this mess."

Tom's eyes darted frantically, searching for an escape route. There, just ahead—a narrow alleyway between two brick buildings. Without hesitation, he ducked into the shadowy passage, his breath coming in ragged gasps.

The alley was a cluttered obstacle course of overflowing dumpsters and discarded cardboard boxes. The stench of rotting garbage assaulted his nostrils as he picked his way through the detritus. Rusty fire escapes clung to the buildings on either side, their ladders tantalizingly out of reach.

"Come on, there's got to be a way out," Tom muttered, his voice betraying a hint of desperation. He could hear the echoing shouts of his pursuers growing closer.

As he rounded a corner, his heart sank. A solid brick wall loomed before him, at least twelve feet high. Tom's hands clenched into fists, his nails digging into his palms.

"No, no, no," he hissed, spinning around to face the way he'd come. "This can't be happening. Not now, not when I'm so close."

The sound of running footsteps grew louder. Tom's eyes darted wildly around the alley, searching for anything that might offer salvation. His gaze settled on a stack of wooden pallets leaning against one wall.

"It's not exactly a golden ticket," he thought, "but it'll have to do."

With a grunt of effort, Tom began dragging the pallets towards the dead end. His muscles screamed in protest, but the adrenaline coursing through his veins gave him strength he didn't know he possessed.

"Come on, Beauchamp," he urged himself. "You didn't come this far to get caught now. Think of the beach in Bali, the Mai Tais, the—"

A voice cut through his desperate musings. "BEAUCHAMP! We know you're down there. Give yourself up!"

Tom's heart raced even faster. He had to move, and fast.

Tom's eyes darted upward, catching sight of a rusted fire escape ladder just within reach. Without hesitation, he leapt, his fingers grasping the cold metal rungs.

"Sorry, fellas," he muttered under his breath, "but I've got a date with destiny that I can't miss."

As he began to climb, the ladder creaked ominously. Tom winced, his knuckles turning white as he gripped tighter. Each step sent a jolt of anxiety through him, the fear of the ladder giving way battling with his desperation to escape.

"Come on, you old piece of junk," he whispered encouragingly to the ladder. "Just a few more feet."

His feet scrambled for purchase, his usually meticulous nature giving way to raw survival instinct. As he climbed higher, the sounds of pursuit grew fainter, replaced by the whistle of wind between the buildings.

Finally, with a final heave, Tom pulled himself onto the rooftop. He collapsed onto his back, chest heaving, the cool concrete a stark contrast to his sweat-soaked shirt.

"I'm getting too old for this," he gasped, staring up at the night sky.

After a moment, Tom pushed himself to his feet, his legs wobbling slightly. He made his way to the edge of the roof, taking in the panoramic view of the city spread out before him.

The cityscape twinkled with a thousand lights, a stark contrast to the darkness he'd just escaped. In the distance, he could hear the wail of sirens, a reminder that his ordeal wasn't over yet.

"What a mess," Tom sighed, running a hand through his graying hair. "This wasn't part of the plan. None of this was part of the plan."

He closed his eyes, trying to steady his racing thoughts. When he opened them again, his gaze was drawn to the distant harbor, where he could just make out the silhouettes of ships against the night sky.

"Maybe," he mused aloud, a hint of his usual calculated tone returning, "it's time for a change of scenery. After all, I've always wanted to see the world."

With renewed determination, Tom turned away from the edge, his mind already formulating his next move. The game wasn't over yet, not by a long shot.

The rooftop door burst open with a thunderous crash, startling Tom from his reverie. Sergeant Jean-Guy Tremblay emerged, his gun drawn and aimed squarely at Tom's chest. The sergeant's eyes blazed with determination, his jaw set in a hard line.

"Freeze, Beauchamp!" Tremblay barked, his voice echoing across the rooftop. "It's over. You've got nowhere left to run."

Tom's heart hammered in his chest as he raised his hands slowly. "Now, now, Sergeant," he said, his voice steady despite his internal panic. "Let's not do anything rash."

Tremblay took a step forward, his gun unwavering. "Save it, Tom. You've led us on quite a chase, but it ends here."

Tom's eyes darted around, desperately searching for an escape route. His gaze landed on a nearby ventilation shaft, and his quick mind began to formulate a plan.

"You know, Jean-Guy," Tom said, inching subtly towards the shaft, "I always admired your dedication. In another life, we might have been friends."

Tremblay scoffed. "In another life, you might have been an honest man. Now, hands behind your head!"

As the sergeant took another step forward, Tom made his move. He lunged for the ventilation shaft, his heart in his throat.

A shot rang out, the bullet whizzing past Tom's ear. He could feel the heat of its passage as he scrambled towards the shaft.

"Dammit, Beauchamp!" Tremblay shouted, firing again.

Tom dove headfirst into the shaft, the metal grate clanging behind him. As he slid into the darkness, he couldn't help but think, "Giselle's going to kill me if the sergeant doesn't get to me first."

With a final burst of energy, Tom squeezed himself into the ventilation shaft, his body barely fitting through the narrow opening. The sound of Sergeant Tremblay's frustrated shout echoed behind him.

"Tabarnac!" Tremblay's voice reverberated through the metal. "You can't hide forever, Beauchamp!"

Tom allowed himself a small, breathless chuckle. "Watch me," he muttered under his breath, pushing himself deeper into the darkness.

As he crawled through the cramped space, dust and cobwebs clung to his face. The shaft was pitch black, forcing Tom to rely on touch alone. His hands fumbled along the cool metal, searching for a path forward.

"Well, Tom," he whispered to himself, "you wanted excitement in your golden years. Be careful what you wish for."

His labored breathing seemed deafening in the confined space. Each inhale brought a fresh wave of musty air, making him fight the urge to cough. The walls pressed in on all sides, and for a moment, panic threatened to overwhelm him.

"Come on, old boy," Tom encouraged himself, his voice barely audible. "You didn't come this far to get stuck in a glorified air duct."

As he inched forward, the sound of his heartbeat pounding in his ears, Tom couldn't help but reflect on the absurdity of his situation. Here he was, a former brake pad factory owner, now crawling through ventilation shafts like some sort of geriatric action hero.

"Giselle always said I had a flair for the dramatic," he mused, a wry smile playing on his lips despite the circumstances. "Though I doubt this is what she had in mind for our retirement."

The shaft suddenly branched off in two directions. Tom paused, considering his options. "Eeny, meeny, miny, moe," he whispered, then chuckled softly. "Oh, who am I kidding? It's all the same in this blasted maze."

He chose the left path, hoping it would lead him to freedom – or at least, away from the determined Sergeant Tremblay.

With a final grunt of effort, Tom pushed against the grate at the end of the ventilation shaft. It gave way with a rusty groan, and he tumbled out onto the rooftop of a neighboring building. The cool night air hit his face, and he gasped, gulping it down greedily.

"Sweet freedom," he muttered, sprawling on his back and staring up at the star-studded sky. His chest heaved as he caught his breath, a mixture of relief and triumph washing over him. "Never thought I'd be so happy to see smog."

After a moment, Tom sat up, his joints creaking in protest. He surveyed his surroundings, taking in the glittering cityscape spread out before him. The distant wail of sirens reminded him that he wasn't out of danger yet.

"Well, Tom," he said to himself, brushing dust off his clothes, "you've really done it this time, haven't you? From brake pads to rooftops in one fell swoop."

He stood up, wincing slightly. "Probably should've stretched before my impromptu acrobatics act."

Tom walked to the edge of the roof, peering down at the streets below. The city pulsed with life, oblivious to his predicament. He took a deep breath, his mind racing with possibilities.

"Alright, think," he muttered, running a hand through his graying hair. "What would James Bond do? Besides order a martini, of course."

He chuckled at his own joke, then grew serious. "I need to lay low, regroup. Can't risk going home, that'll be the first place they look."

Tom's eyes scanned the horizon, settling on a neon sign for a cheap motel a few blocks away. "Not exactly the Ritz, but it'll have to do."

He squared his shoulders, a look of determination settling on his weathered face. "This isn't over yet. I've come too far to give up now."

With one last glance at the city lights, Tom made his way towards the roof access door. "Time to disappear for a while, old boy. The game's still afoot."

As Tom approached the roof access door, he paused, his hand hovering over the handle. The faint sound of sirens in the distance made his heart race.

"Easy now," he whispered to himself, "one step at a time."

He opened the door cautiously, peering down the dimly lit stairwell. The coast seemed clear. Tom began his descent, each step echoing softly in the empty space.

"From factory owner to fugitive," he mused, a wry smile playing on his lips. "Mom always said I had a flair for the dramatic."

Reaching the ground floor, Tom paused to listen. The lobby appeared deserted. He straightened his rumpled clothes and tried to adopt a casual air.

"Just act natural," he muttered. "You're just a tired businessman heading home after a long day. Nothing suspicious here."

As he stepped out onto the sidewalk, the cool night air hit his face. Tom glanced left and right, then set off towards the motel, his pace brisk but measured.

"I wonder if Sergeant Tremblay is still fuming on that rooftop," he thought, allowing himself a small chuckle. "Sorry, Jean-Guy, but this cat's got a few more lives left."

The neon sign of the motel grew closer, its flickering light a beacon of temporary safety. Tom felt a mix of exhaustion and exhilaration coursing through his veins.

"One night to recharge, then it's back to the drawing board," he resolved. "This game's far from over, and I've still got a few tricks up my sleeve."

With a final glance over his shoulder, Tom disappeared into the shadows of the motel entrance, leaving behind only the echo of his footsteps and the promise of more adventures to come.

Chapter 13

CRASH!

Tom's eyes flew open, his heart leaping into his throat. The deafening sound reverberated through the house, shattering the peaceful silence of the night. For a split second, he wondered if he was dreaming, but the rapid thudding of his pulse told him otherwise.

"What the—" he muttered, his voice thick with sleep. As he pushed himself up on his elbows, the familiar creak of the bedroom floorboards reached his ears, followed by something far more ominous: heavy footsteps, multiple sets, moving with purpose through his home.

Oh God, Tom thought, his mind spinning into overdrive. This is it. They're here.

He could hear voices now, gruff and authoritative, calling out commands. "Clear!" echoed from somewhere downstairs, followed by the thunderous sound of more doors being forced open.

Tom's fingers gripped the edge of the mattress, his knuckles turning white. He'd always known this day might come, had even rehearsed it in his mind countless times. But now that it was here, he felt woefully unprepared.

"Giselle," he whispered, reaching out to shake his wife awake. But his hand met only empty space. Right, he remembered. She'd gone to sleep in the guest room after their argument last night.

The footsteps were getting closer now, ascending the stairs with a deliberate, menacing rhythm. Tom's eyes darted around the room, searching for... what? A way out? A magical solution to fix this mess he'd created?

"I should have listened to her," he muttered to himself, a wry smile twisting his lips despite the gravity of the situation. "Counterfeit currency... what was I thinking?"

But he knew exactly what he'd been thinking. Years of struggling, of watching his dreams slip away, of feeling the weight of failure pressing down on him. He'd seen an opportunity, a chance to finally get ahead, and he'd taken it. Now, as the sound of approaching doom echoed through his home, Tom couldn't help but wonder if it had all been worth it.

The bedroom door burst open, flooding the room with harsh light. Tom squinted, raising a hand to shield his eyes, his heart pounding so hard he was sure it would burst from his chest at any moment.

"Thomas Beauchamp," a stern voice barked. "You are under arrest."

As the officers swarmed into the room, Tom let out a long, resigned sigh. Well, he thought, I guess this is what they mean by 'get rich or die trying'.

Tom's heart hammered in his chest as he scrambled out of bed, his bare feet hitting the cold hardwood floor. His eyes darted frantically around the room, searching for any hiding spot that might conceal the damning evidence.

"Think, Tom, think!" he muttered to himself, running a shaky hand through his graying hair. The sound of heavy footsteps echoed through the house, growing louder with each passing second.

He lunged for the dresser, yanking open drawers and rifling through their contents. Socks, underwear, and old t-shirts flew through the air as he searched for the envelope containing the counterfeit bills.

"Where did I put them?" Tom hissed, his voice barely above a whisper. "Come on, you meticulous idiot. You had a plan for this!"

As he rushed out of the bedroom and down the hallway, Tom's mind raced, considering and discarding potential hiding spots with lightning speed. The attic? Too obvious. The garage? Too far. The toilet tank? Too cliché.

He paused at the top of the stairs, gripping the banister as a wave of dizziness washed over him. "Okay, Tom," he coached himself, taking a deep breath. "You've planned for every contingency. Time to put those skills to use."

His eyes landed on the ancient grandfather clock in the corner of the living room. A faint glimmer of hope sparked in his chest. "Perfect," he breathed, a grim smile tugging at his lips. "Who says you can't turn back time?"

"Tom? Tom, what's happening?" Giselle's voice, tinged with fear and confusion, cut through the chaos of Tom's racing thoughts.

His heart skipped a beat. Giselle. In his frantic search for a hiding spot, he'd momentarily forgotten about her. Tom's stomach churned with a mixture of guilt and renewed panic.

"Giselle, stay where you are!" he called back, his voice strained as he tried to sound calm. "Everything's going to be fine!"

Tom's eyes darted between the grandfather clock and the hallway leading to their bedroom. He could hear Giselle's footsteps, hesitant but drawing nearer. His mind whirled, torn between securing the evidence and protecting the woman he loved.

"Tom, there are people outside. I think they're police!" Giselle's voice quavered, her soft Quebecois accent more pronounced in her distress.

"I know, chérie," Tom replied, his tone gentle despite the urgency coursing through him. "Just... just give me a moment. Don't come out yet."

He moved towards the clock, every muscle in his body taut with tension. 'Protect Giselle, hide the evidence, find a way out,' he repeated in his head like a mantra. The weight of responsibility pressed down on him, threatening to crush his resolve.

"What have you done?" Giselle's question, barely above a whisper, hit Tom like a physical blow.

He turned to see her standing in the doorway, her striking red hair disheveled, her green eyes wide with a mixture of fear and dawning realization. In that moment, Tom knew he had to make a choice – and fast.

Tom's heart raced as he made his decision. With practiced precision, he knelt by the antique coffee table, his fingers finding the hidden latch beneath its ornate edge. The secret compartment in the floorboards sprang open, revealing a dark cavity.

"I'm sorry, Giselle," Tom muttered, more to himself than to her, as he hastily shoved the stack of counterfeit bills into the hiding spot. His hands trembled slightly, betraying the adrenaline surging through his veins.

As he carefully replaced the floorboard, Tom's mind raced. 'This wasn't how it was supposed to go,' he thought ruefully. 'All that planning, all those sleepless nights...'

The sound of heavy footsteps echoed from the hallway, growing louder with each passing second. Tom's breath caught in his throat as he realized time was running out.

"Honey," he said, his voice surprisingly steady as he stood up, smoothing down his rumpled pajamas, "whatever happens, remember I love you."

Tom's eyes scanned the room, ensuring nothing was out of place. He took a deep breath, willing his racing heart to slow. 'Just another Tuesday morning,' he told himself, trying to summon the nonchalance of a man with nothing to hide.

As the footsteps reached the door, Tom plastered what he hoped was a convincing look of confused innocence on his face. He turned towards the entrance, ready to face whatever came next, all while silently praying his hidden compartment would keep its secrets.

The door exploded inward with a thunderous crash, splintering wood flying through the air. A flood of uniformed officers poured into the room, their weapons drawn and faces set with grim determination.

At the forefront stood Sergeant Jean-Guy Tremblay, his muscular frame filling the doorway. His salt-and-pepper hair caught the early morning light as his sharp eyes locked onto Tom.

"Tom Beauchamp!" Tremblay's voice boomed, cutting through the chaos. "On the ground, now!"

Tom's mind reeled, but his body responded automatically. He dropped to his knees, then lay flat on his stomach, feeling the cool hardwood against his cheek. His heart hammered so loudly he was sure everyone in the room could hear it.

"Hands behind your back!" Tremblay barked, moving swiftly towards Tom.

As Tom complied, he couldn't help but think, 'This is it. Everything I've worked for, gone in an instant.' He felt the cold metal of handcuffs snap around his wrists, the finality of the sound sending a chill down his spine.

"Tom Beauchamp, you're under arrest for suspicion of counterfeiting," Tremblay announced, his tone leaving no room for argument.

Tom's mind raced, desperately searching for a way out. 'Maybe I can talk my way out of this,' he thought. 'Or maybe... maybe there's still a chance to run.'

But as he was hauled to his feet, surrounded by stern-faced officers, the gravity of his situation sank in. Tom's eyes darted around the room, taking in the scene of his carefully constructed life crumbling around him.

As the officers methodically searched the house, Tom's mind spiraled into a frenzy of exaggerated scenarios. He imagined himself in a striped prison uniform, chipping away at rocks with a tiny pickaxe. 'Great, I've gone from brake pads to breaking rocks. At least I'm still in manufacturing,' he thought wryly, suppressing a hysterical chuckle.

His gaze darted around the room, watching the officers rifling through his belongings. 'Oh, fantastic. They're probably going to confiscate my prized collection of novelty staplers. What will I use to fasten my prison memoirs now?'

Suddenly, a commotion from the hallway caught Tom's attention. His heart sank as he saw Giselle being led into the room, her vibrant red hair disheveled and her green eyes wide with fear.

"Tom!" she cried out, her voice trembling. "What's happening?"

Tom's protective instincts kicked in, momentarily overriding his panic. "It's okay, Giselle," he said softly, trying to keep his voice steady. "We're going to get through this together. I promise."

Giselle's eyes locked with his, searching for reassurance. Tom mustered a small smile, hoping it conveyed more confidence than he felt. "Remember when we got lost in that corn maze last fall? This is just like that, only with more handcuffs and less corn."

A ghost of a smile flickered across Giselle's face, but her worry was still evident. "But Tom, what about-"

"Shh," Tom interrupted gently, acutely aware of the officers around them. "We'll figure it out. We always do."

As Giselle was led to sit on the couch, Tom's mind raced again. 'Well, this isn't exactly how I planned our morning to go. Coffee and croissants would've been nicer than cuffs and cops.'

Tom's thoughts were interrupted by a sharp cracking sound. He turned to see two officers prying up the floorboards in the living room, revealing the hidden compartment he had painstakingly constructed. His heart pounded so loudly he was sure everyone in the room could hear it.

"What do we have here?" one of the officers called out, shining a flashlight into the dark space.

Tom held his breath, his palms sweating. 'Please don't find the bills, please don't find the bills,' he chanted silently, his eyes darting between the officers and Giselle.

To his immense relief, the officers seemed more interested in a stack of documents tucked away in the corner of the compartment. Tom exhaled slowly, careful not to draw attention to himself.

"Looks like we've got some interesting paperwork here, Sergeant," the officer announced, pulling out the files.

As the officers pored over the documents, Sergeant Tremblay approached Tom and Giselle. "Mr. Beauchamp, Ms. Tremblay, you're both under arrest," he stated firmly.

Tom felt the cold metal of handcuffs closing around his wrists. He glanced at Giselle, who was receiving the same treatment. Her face was pale, but her jaw was set in determination.

"Well, Giselle," Tom said, trying to inject some levity into the situation, "I always wanted to take you out in style, but this isn't quite what I had in mind."

Giselle managed a weak smile. "At least we match," she replied, nodding towards their handcuffs.

As they were led out of the house, Tom blinked in the harsh morning light. Police cars with flashing lights lined the street, and a crowd of curious neighbors had gathered to watch the spectacle.

"Oh, look," Tom muttered to Giselle, "we're putting on a show for the whole neighborhood. I hope they appreciate our impromptu performance."

The officers guided Tom and Giselle towards separate police vehicles. As they approached the cars, Tom's heart raced, his mind frantically searching for a way to reassure Giselle. He turned his head, catching her eye just as an officer opened the car door.

"Stay strong, ma chérie," Tom called out, his voice cracking slightly. "We'll get through this."

Giselle's green eyes locked onto his, a whirlpool of emotions swirling within them. "Je t'aime, Tom," she responded, her soft voice carrying a tremor of fear.

As the officer gently pushed Tom's head down to guide him into the backseat, he caught one last glimpse of Giselle. Her fiery red hair glinted in the morning sun, a stark contrast to the somber situation. In that fleeting moment, Tom saw a flicker of the determination that had first drawn him to her.

'We've gotten out of tighter spots than this,' Tom thought to himself, trying to summon his usual optimism. 'Well, maybe not quite this tight, but...'

The car door slammed shut, cutting off his view of Giselle. Tom leaned back against the seat, the cool leather a stark reminder of his new reality. He closed his eyes, took a deep breath, and muttered, "Well, Tom, you wanted excitement in your golden years. Be careful what you wish for, I suppose."

Chapter 14

The cold concrete wall pressed against Tom's back as he sat alone in his jail cell, the harsh fluorescent lights casting a sickly glow on his weary face. He ran his fingers through his graying hair, wincing as he felt the coarse strands—a stark reminder of how much his ambitious scheme had aged him.

"Well, Tommy boy," he muttered to himself, a wry smile tugging at the corner of his lips, "you've really done it this time, haven't you?"

He shifted on the hard metal bench, trying to find a comfortable position. The clanging of cell doors echoed through the corridor, punctuating the oppressive silence.

Tom let out a heavy sigh. "Let's see, what are my options here? Door number one: plead guilty and hope for leniency. Door number two: fight it out in court and risk a longer sentence. Or door number three: break out using my extensive knowledge of prison architecture gleaned from watching 'The Shawshank Redemption' seventeen times."

He chuckled softly at his own joke, the sound bouncing off the bare walls. His eyes drifted to the small barred window, a sliver of the outside world taunting him with its freedom.

"I wonder what would have happened if those bills had actually made it into circulation," Tom mused, his mind conjuring up increasingly absurd scenarios. "The entire economy thrown into chaos, the dollar becoming as worthless as Monopoly money. And there I'd be, sitting on a throne made of counterfeit cash, laughing maniacally like some B-movie villain."

He shook his head, his expression sobering. "No, no. That's not who you are, Tom. You're just a guy who wanted a better life, who took a chance and... well, royally screwed it up."

The sound of footsteps approaching his cell made Tom straighten up, his face automatically assuming a more composed expression. As the guard passed by without stopping, Tom relaxed again, letting out a breath he didn't realize he'd been holding.

"One thing's for sure," he said to himself, his voice barely above a whisper, "I'm never going to look at a dollar bill the same way again."

Tom's thoughts drifted to Giselle, her vibrant red hair and sparkling green eyes vivid in his mind. A wry smile played on his lips as he imagined her reaction to his illicit activities.

"Oh, mon Dieu, Tom!" he mimicked her Quebecois accent, chuckling softly. "You turned our basement into a counterfeiting operation? I thought you were just really into scrapbooking!"

He could almost hear her exasperated sigh, picturing her hands on her hips, those expressive eyes flashing with a mix of disbelief and reluctant amusement.

"You know, chéri," Tom continued his imaginary conversation, "I was just trying to provide for us. A little fraud here, a touch of racketeering there..."

He shook his head, his smile fading. "She deserved better than this," he murmured, running a hand through his graying hair.

Tom's gaze drifted to the ceiling, his mind racing with possibilities. "If it had worked, though," he mused, "We could've had it all. A villa in the south of France, maybe. Giselle sipping champagne by the pool, me finally learning how to pronounce 'croissant' properly."

He sighed, the weight of reality settling back on his shoulders. "But at what cost?" Tom asked himself, his voice barely audible. "How many people would've suffered because of my 'grand plan'? How many lives disrupted?"

The flickering fluorescent light above cast dancing shadows on the cell walls, reminding Tom of the precarious nature of his scheme. "It was all smoke and mirrors," he admitted to himself. "A house of cards waiting to topple."

Tom chuckled softly, shaking his head at his own folly. "Oh, woe is me!" he exclaimed dramatically, raising a hand to his forehead. "What a tangled web we weave, when first we practice to deceive... and print fake money in our basement."

He couldn't help but laugh at the absurdity of it all. Here he was, Tom Beauchamp, erstwhile businessman turned would-be counterfeiter, languishing in a jail cell like some modern-day Hamlet. "To print, or not to print," he mused aloud, "that is the question."

His laughter echoed off the concrete walls, a touch of hysteria creeping in at the edges. "Oh, how the mighty have fallen," Tom declared to his imaginary audience. "From captain of industry to jailbird extraordinaire. What a plot twist!"

As his chuckles subsided, Tom's mind drifted back to his days at the brake pad factory. The familiar hum of machinery filled his ears, a comforting rhythm that had once been the soundtrack to his life.

"You know," he said to no one in particular, "there was a time when I thought the height of excitement was perfecting the friction coefficient on a new pad design."

He closed his eyes, remembering the satisfaction of a job well done, the pride in providing a quality product. "Who would've thought I'd trade in brake pads for funny money?" Tom mused. "Talk about a career change."

The irony wasn't lost on him. "All I wanted was a little more comfort," he sighed. "A nicer house, maybe a vacation once in a while. Instead, I've got three hots and a cot courtesy of Uncle Sam."

Tom shook his head, a wry smile playing on his lips. "I guess you could say I've really put the brakes on my life now, huh?"

Tom's thoughts wandered to the colorful cast of characters he'd encountered during his foray into counterfeiting. One face stood out among the rest: Patrice Dubois, the smooth-talking Frenchman who'd become his unlikely mentor in the world of financial crime.

"Ah, Patrice," Tom chuckled to himself, running a hand through his graying hair. "What I wouldn't give for one of your philosophical ramblings right about now."

He could almost hear Patrice's refined accent echoing in his cell. "Mon ami," Tom mimicked, "morality is but a construct of the bourgeoisie. We are merely redistributing wealth, non?"

Tom snorted, shaking his head. "Yeah, redistributing it right into our pockets."

He recalled a particularly memorable conversation they'd had over expensive cognac in a dimly lit Parisian bar. Patrice had leaned in, blue eyes twinkling mischievously as he'd said, "Thomas, my boy, think of us as modern-day Robin Hoods. We take from the rich... and give to ourselves."

"And look where that Robin Hood routine got me," Tom muttered, gesturing at his surroundings. "Trading cognac for prison hooch."

As the humor faded, a sobering realization settled over Tom like a heavy blanket. He stared at his hands, imagining them filled with the counterfeit bills he'd so meticulously crafted.

"Christ," he whispered, the weight of his actions finally sinking in. "What if those had actually made it into circulation?"

Tom's mind raced, conjuring images of economic chaos: stock markets crashing, banks failing, people's life savings rendered worthless overnight. The stability he'd taken for granted his entire life suddenly seemed frighteningly fragile.

"All because I wanted a bigger slice of the pie," he murmured, a newfound appreciation for the humble dollar bill washing over him. "Who knew a little green piece of paper could hold the world together?"

Tom leaned his head back against the cold concrete wall, his eyes tracing the cracks in the ceiling as his mind wandered to the future. The possibilities stretched out before him like an uncharted map, filled with both promise and peril.

"What now, Beauchamp?" he asked himself aloud, his voice echoing slightly in the small cell. "Can't exactly go back to selling brake pads after this little adventure."

He chuckled wryly, picturing himself behind a counter, trying to peddle auto parts to unsuspecting customers. "Sorry, sir, we're all out of genuine parts. How about some counterfeit ones instead?"

The humor faded as quickly as it had come, replaced by a sobering realization. Tom sat up straighter, his brow furrowed in concentration.

"No more shortcuts," he said firmly, as if making a vow to himself. "Time to do things the right way, even if it's the hard way."

He thought back to his days running the brake pad factory, remembering the satisfaction of honest work and the pride he'd felt in building something real. It hadn't been glamorous, but it had been his.

"Maybe that's the lesson here," Tom mused, running a hand through his graying hair. "Success doesn't have to mean private jets and champagne. It's about building something meaningful, something that lasts."

As he spoke the words aloud, Tom felt a weight lift from his shoulders. For the first time since his arrest, a genuine smile tugged at the corners of his mouth.

"Alright, Tom," he said, standing up and pacing the small cell. "Time to take a good, hard look in the mirror."

He stopped, facing his reflection in the small, scratched metal surface above the sink. The man staring back at him looked older, wearier, but there was a glimmer of something in his eyes – determination, perhaps, or hope.

"I've made a real mess of things, haven't I?" Tom said to his reflection. "Hurt a lot of people along the way. Giselle, the guys at the factory, hell, even the poor saps who would've ended up with my funny money."

He took a deep breath, squaring his shoulders. "Time to own up to it all. Make things right, as much as I can."

The resolve in his voice surprised even him. It was as if speaking the words aloud had made them real, solidifying his commitment to change.

Tom leaned against the cold concrete wall, his eyes fixed on a spot on the floor. The humor that had sustained him earlier had faded, replaced by a sobering realization.

"Even when I'm out of here," he muttered, "this isn't over. Not by a long shot."

He closed his eyes, envisioning the challenges that lay ahead. Legal battles, damaged relationships, a tarnished reputation - the consequences of his actions stretched far beyond the confines of his cell.

"I'll probably be paying lawyers for years," Tom said with a bitter chuckle. "And that's if I'm lucky enough to avoid more jail time."

He ran his fingers along the rough surface of the wall, the texture grounding him in the present moment. The weight of his choices pressed down on him, heavier than ever before.

"God, what a mess," he sighed. "I wanted financial freedom, but all I've done is shackle myself with more debt and guilt than I ever had before."

Tom's gaze drifted to the barred window, a sliver of sky visible beyond. The world out there seemed vast and daunting now, full of consequences he'd have to face.

"It's not just about me anymore," he realized aloud. "Every fake bill I printed could have hurt someone. Businesses, families... I didn't think it through."

As the gravity of his actions sank in, Tom felt a shift within himself. The ambitious schemer was giving way to something else - a man ready to face the music.

He took a deep breath, filling his lungs with the stale cell air. As he exhaled, Tom felt a strange sense of clarity wash over him.

"You know what?" he said to the empty cell. "This... this might be exactly what I needed."

Tom stood up, stretching his stiff muscles. "A wake-up call. A chance to hit the reset button."

He began to pace, his steps matching the rhythm of his thoughts. "I can't change what I've done, but I can change where I go from here."

Tom stopped, a look of determination crossing his face. "Time to grow up, Tommy boy. No more get-rich-quick schemes. No more cutting corners."

He nodded to himself, as if sealing a pact. "I'm going to make this right. Whatever it takes."

Tom squared his shoulders and walked to the cell door, his footsteps echoing in the confined space. He gripped the cold metal bars, peering out into the dimly lit corridor.

"Guard?" he called out, his voice steadier than he expected. "I'd like to speak with someone about my case, please."

As he waited for a response, Tom's mind raced with possibilities. He muttered to himself, "Maybe I can cooperate, provide information. It won't undo what I've done, but it's a start."

The sound of approaching footsteps made Tom straighten up. He ran a hand through his graying hair, aware of how he must look – a middle-aged man in a jumpsuit, far from the successful businessman he'd once imagined himself to be.

"Mr. Beauchamp," the guard said, arriving at his cell. "You wanted to talk?"

Tom nodded, meeting the guard's eyes. "Yes, I've been doing some thinking. A lot of thinking, actually. I want to make things right."

The guard raised an eyebrow, clearly having heard similar declarations before. But something in Tom's tone must have resonated, because he nodded slowly.

"I'll see what I can do," the guard said. "In the meantime, chin up, Beauchamp. It's not the end of the world."

As the guard walked away, Tom returned to his cot, sitting down with a mix of nervousness and hope. He glanced at the small patch of sky visible through his window, a faint smile tugging at his lips.

"No," he whispered to himself, "it's not the end. It's a new beginning."

Chapter 15

Tom Beauchamp shifted uncomfortably in the plush leather chair, his weary eyes fixed on Rosalie Bélanger as she paced behind her imposing mahogany desk. The faint scent of lemon polish hung in the air, a stark contrast to the tension building in the room.

"A technicality?" Tom's voice cracked, betraying his skepticism. "Rosalie, I appreciate your efforts, but this sounds like grasping at straws."

Rosalie's piercing blue eyes locked onto Tom's, her petite frame radiating an aura of unwavering confidence. "I assure you, Tom, this is far from a desperate attempt. It's our golden ticket."

Tom's mind raced, recalling the meticulous planning that had led him to this point. How could a simple glitch be his salvation? It seemed too good to be true, and in his experience, such things usually were.

Rosalie's heels clicked sharply against the hardwood floor as she moved to retrieve a folder from her desk. "Let me present the evidence, and you'll see why this is our best shot at proving your innocence."

Tom leaned forward, his curiosity piqued despite his reservations. He watched intently as Rosalie spread out several documents and photographs on the desk between them.

"Here," she said, pointing to a series of time-stamped images. "Do you notice anything unusual?"

Tom squinted, studying the grainy surveillance footage. At first glance, nothing seemed out of the ordinary. But as he looked closer, he noticed a slight jump in the time stamp.

"There's a gap," he murmured, more to himself than to Rosalie.

"Exactly," Rosalie replied, a hint of triumph in her voice. "A glitch in the surveillance system caused a brief interruption in the footage during the crucial moment of the cash handoff."

Tom's heart raced. Could this really be the break he needed? He'd spent countless nights planning every detail of his scheme, yet he'd never anticipated that a technical malfunction could be his saving grace.

"But how does this prove my innocence?" Tom asked, his tone a mixture of hope and lingering doubt.

Rosalie's lips curved into a confident smile. "It creates reasonable doubt, Tom. Without clear footage of the actual handoff, the prosecution's case becomes significantly weaker. We can argue that the glitch could have concealed exculpatory evidence."

Tom nodded slowly, processing the information. It was a sliver of hope, but in his current situation, even the smallest opening seemed like a godsend.

"I see the wheels turning, Tom," Rosalie said, her voice softer now. "This technicality could be our ticket to proving your innocence. It's not a guarantee, but it's a fighting chance."

As Tom contemplated the potential of this unexpected development, he couldn't help but marvel at Rosalie's sharp mind. She truly was several steps ahead, just as her reputation suggested.

"Well, Rosalie," Tom said, a hint of his old determination creeping back into his voice, "I suppose it's time we make the most of this glitch, isn't it?"

Rosalie's eyes lit up with a mischievous glint. "Now you're talking, Tom. Let's brainstorm some ideas to really throw law enforcement for a loop."

Tom leaned forward in his chair, his fatigue momentarily forgotten. "What did you have in mind?"

"Well," Rosalie began, tapping her manicured nails on the polished desk, "we need something unexpected, something that'll make them question everything they think they know."

Tom's mind raced, years of meticulous planning kicking into overdrive. "What if we... created a decoy cash drop?" he suggested, his voice hesitant but gaining confidence.

Rosalie raised an eyebrow. "Go on."

"We could stage a fake handoff," Tom continued, gesturing animatedly. "Make it look like I was actually passing off, I don't know, movie props or something equally innocuous."

A chuckle escaped Rosalie's lips. "Movie props? That's certainly creative, Tom. But we might need something a bit more... outrageous."

Tom's brow furrowed as he considered wilder options. "How about we claim I was actually undercover, working with a secret government agency?"

Rosalie snorted, her professional demeanor cracking slightly. "Oh, that's rich. Tom Beauchamp, brake pad mogul turned secret agent. I can see the headlines now."

Despite the gravity of his situation, Tom found himself grinning. This brainstorming session was taking an unexpectedly entertaining turn. "Alright, how about this: we say the cash was actually for a surprise party for the arresting officer's birthday?"

Rosalie burst into laughter, her carefully styled hair shaking as she doubled over. "Oh, Tom," she gasped between giggles, "you're really getting into the spirit of this, aren't you?"

Tom couldn't help but join in the laughter, feeling a strange mix of desperation and amusement. As absurd as these ideas were, they were the first glimmer of hope he'd had in weeks.

As their laughter subsided, Tom's eyes suddenly lit up with an idea. He leaned forward in his chair, his voice dropping to a conspiratorial whisper. "What if... what if I disguised myself as a janitor and snuck into the police station to tamper with the evidence?"

Rosalie's mirth vanished instantly, replaced by a look of concern. "Tom, that's far too risky. We can't possibly—"

"No, no, hear me out," Tom interrupted, his hands gesticulating wildly. "I could slip in unnoticed, find the evidence room, and... well, do something to muddy the waters."

Rosalie pursed her lips, her sharp mind already dissecting the idea. "It's completely illegal, not to mention dangerous. If you're caught—"

"But I won't be," Tom insisted, his eyes gleaming with a determination Rosalie hadn't seen since their first meeting. "I'll be careful, meticulous. You know how I am with planning."

Rosalie sighed, pinching the bridge of her nose. "Tom, your enthusiasm is... admirable, but this isn't like running a brake pad factory. The stakes are much higher."

Tom leaned back, a wry smile playing on his lips. "Higher stakes, higher rewards, right? Isn't that what you always say?"

Rosalie's eyes narrowed, recognizing her own words being used against her. She studied Tom's face, noting the spark of life that had been missing for weeks. Despite her better judgment, she found herself warming to the idea.

"Fine," she conceded, holding up a warning finger. "But we do this my way. You'll need training."

Tom's face split into a wide grin. "Training? Like in those heist movies?"

Rosalie couldn't help but chuckle. "Something like that. Let's start with the basics of janitorial work."

Rosalie strode into her office, a large paper bag clutched in her hands. Tom looked up from the police station blueprints spread across her desk, his eyebrows raising in curiosity.

"Is that what I think it is?" he asked, a mix of excitement and apprehension in his voice.

Rosalie nodded, emptying the contents of the bag onto her leather couch. A janitor's uniform tumbled out, followed by an assortment of cleaning supplies.

"It's all here," she said, her tone businesslike. "Uniform, mop, bucket, cleaning solutions. Even got you a pair of non-slip shoes."

Tom picked up the uniform, holding it against himself. "How'd you get my size so spot-on?"

Rosalie smirked. "I'm a lawyer, Tom. Attention to detail is my bread and butter."

As Tom examined the cleaning supplies, Rosalie unfolded a detailed map of the police station on her desk. "Now, let's go over the layout one more time," she said, her finger tracing a path through the corridors.

Tom leaned in, his brow furrowed in concentration. "Right, so I enter through the back entrance here," he muttered, pointing at the map.

"Exactly," Rosalie nodded. "The night shift change happens at 11 PM. That's your window to slip in unnoticed."

Tom's hand trembled slightly as he traced the route to the evidence room. "What if I run into someone?"

Rosalie's blue eyes locked onto his. "Remember your training. Head down, quiet 'evening,' and keep moving. You're invisible, just part of the background."

Tom took a deep breath, steeling himself. "Right, invisible. I can do that."

As the clock struck 10:30 PM, Tom found himself outside the police station, heart pounding in his chest. He adjusted his janitor's cap, gripping the mop handle like a lifeline.

"Just another night of cleaning," he whispered to himself, mustering up courage. "Nothing suspicious about a janitor doing his job."

With a deep breath, Tom pushed open the back door, wincing at the slight creak. The corridor stretched before him, dimly lit and eerily quiet. He took a tentative step forward, then another, the squeak of his non-slip shoes echoing in the silence.

Just as he rounded the first corner, a door suddenly opened. Tom's heart leapt into his throat as an officer emerged, stifling a yawn.

"Evening," Tom mumbled, keeping his head down as Rosalie had instructed.

The officer gave a distracted nod and continued past, leaving Tom to release a shaky breath.

'That was close,' he thought, his palms sweaty on the mop handle. 'But I'm still here. Still invisible. I can do this.'

With renewed determination, Tom pressed on, each step bringing him closer to his goal – and to potential disaster.

Tom's heart raced as he finally reached the evidence room. He fumbled with the keycard Rosalie had somehow procured, his hands trembling as he swiped it through the reader. The lock clicked open, and he slipped inside, closing the door behind him with a soft thud.

"Alright, Tom," he muttered to himself, scanning the dimly lit room. "You've planned for this. Just find the footage and... do whatever it is you're supposed to do to it."

He located the computer terminal and sat down, staring at the screen with growing apprehension. Buttons, icons, and file names swam before his eyes.

"Come on," he whispered urgently. "It can't be that hard. You ran a whole factory, for crying out loud."

Tom clicked on a folder labeled "Surveillance," then another marked with yesterday's date. A list of video files appeared, and he scrolled through them, searching for the right timestamp.

"Aha!" he exclaimed, then immediately clapped a hand over his mouth, glancing nervously at the door.

As he attempted to open the file, a password prompt appeared. Tom's stomach dropped.

"No, no, no," he groaned. "Think, Tom. What would Rosalie do?"

In a moment of desperation, he typed "password" into the box. To his utter disbelief, it worked.

"You've got to be kidding me," he chuckled, shaking his head.

Just as Tom located the segment of footage he needed to alter, his elbow knocked over a cup of pens on the desk. As he scrambled to catch it, his hand hit a large red button on a nearby console.

Suddenly, an ear-splitting alarm blared through the building. Red lights began flashing, and Tom could hear shouts and running footsteps in the hallway outside.

"Oh, God," he gasped, panic setting in. "What do I do? What do I do?"

Tom burst through the door of Rosalie's office, his janitor's uniform askew and his face flushed. He slammed the door behind him, leaning against it as he gasped for air.

Rosalie jumped up from her desk, eyes wide. "Tom! What on earth—"

"I did it," he wheezed, a manic grin spreading across his face. "Well, sort of. I mean, I didn't actually change anything, but I sure as hell caused a commotion."

Rosalie's jaw dropped as Tom recounted his misadventures. With each detail—the miraculous password guess, the knocked-over pens, the accidental alarm trigger—her expression morphed from shock to disbelief to barely contained amusement.

"You set off the alarm?" she repeated, a snort of laughter escaping despite her best efforts.

Tom nodded, still catching his breath. "I panicked. Started running. Knocked over a mop bucket, slipped in the mess. I think I took out half the evidence room trying to stay upright."

Rosalie doubled over, shoulders shaking with silent laughter. Tom watched her for a moment before joining in, the absurdity of the situation finally hitting him.

"We're terrible criminals," he choked out between guffaws.

"Speak for yourself," Rosalie retorted, wiping tears from her eyes. "I'm an excellent lawyer. You're the one who can't even pull off a simple B&E."

As their laughter subsided, Tom slumped into a chair, running a hand through his disheveled hair. "What were we thinking, Rosalie? This plan was insane from the start."

Rosalie leaned against her desk, her expression softening. "We were thinking we'd do whatever it takes to prove your innocence. It might not have been our finest moment, but at least it shows we're committed."

Tom nodded, a wry smile tugging at his lips. "Committed is one word for it. Certifiable might be another."

"Look," Rosalie said, her tone turning serious, "we knew this wasn't going to be easy. But we're not giving up. We'll find another way to tackle this evidence problem."

Tom's eyes met hers, determination replacing the earlier panic. "You're right. We've come too far to back down now. What's next?"

Rosalie grabbed a legal pad and pen. "First, we need to come up with a solid alibi for your whereabouts tonight. Then, we'll start prepping for the trial. No more amateur hour stunts."

As they began brainstorming, Tom couldn't help but feel a surge of gratitude for Rosalie's unwavering support. Despite the night's chaos, he knew they were in this fight together, come what may.

Tom chuckled, shaking his head as he stood up. "You know, Rosalie, if someone had told me a year ago that I'd be breaking into police stations and masquerading as a janitor, I'd have thought they were crazy."

Rosalie smirked, her blue eyes twinkling with amusement. "And yet here we are, living out your wildest crime drama fantasies. Who knew brake pad manufacturing was such a gateway to a life of excitement?"

"Oh yes, nothing says 'thrilling lifestyle' quite like risking jail time over faulty surveillance footage," Tom quipped, straightening his rumpled shirt. He paused, a thought occurring to him. "Hey, do you think I should add 'proficient in janitorial arts' to my resume?"

Rosalie snorted, gathering her things. "Only if you want to add 'caught red-handed' right after it. Come on, let's get out of here before you get any more bright ideas."

As they made their way to the door, Tom couldn't help but feel a mix of nervousness and exhilaration. Despite the gravity of their situation, there was something oddly freeing about embracing the absurdity of it all.

"You know," he mused, holding the door open for Rosalie, "I never thought I'd say this, but I'm actually looking forward to our next ridiculous scheme. Who knows? Maybe next time we'll pull off a heist dressed as mimes."

Rosalie rolled her eyes, but couldn't suppress a smile. "Let's focus on winning this case first, Tom. Save the mime act for your victory party."

As they stepped into the cool night air, Tom felt a renewed sense of determination. Whatever challenges lay ahead, he knew that with Rosalie by his side – and their unique brand of humor – they were ready to face them head-on.

Chapter 16

Rosalie Bélanger's heels clicked sharply against the polished marble floor as she strode into the packed courtroom. Her piercing blue eyes swept the room, taking in every detail with a practiced efficiency. The murmur of hushed conversations died down as she made her way to the defense table, her tailored charcoal suit a stark contrast to the sea of muted colors surrounding her.

As she set her briefcase on the table with a soft thud, Rosalie allowed herself a small smile. This was her arena, and she was ready for battle. She smoothed an invisible wrinkle from her jacket, her mind already racing through potential strategies.

The courtroom doors swung open again, and Rosalie's gaze snapped to the newcomers. Alessandra Bianchi entered first, her posture radiating determination. Close behind her was Dr. François Girard, his wiry frame nearly lost in an ill-fitting tweed jacket.

"Ah, the dynamic duo arrives," Rosalie muttered under her breath, her lips quirking into a wry smile. She watched as they made their way to the prosecution's table, noting the intense focus in Alessandra's eyes and the slight tremor in Dr. Girard's hands as he clutched his briefcase.

Rosalie leaned back in her chair, crossing her legs as she observed her opponents. "Dr. Girard seems a bit nervous today," she thought, filing away that tidbit for later use. "I wonder what surprises they have in store."

As the bailiff called for all to rise, Rosalie stood smoothly, her confident demeanor a stark contrast to the palpable tension in the room. She caught Alessandra's eye across the aisle and nodded slightly, a gesture of professional respect tinged with a hint of challenge.

"Let the games begin," Rosalie thought, a thrill of anticipation coursing through her veins as the judge entered the courtroom. She took a deep breath, centering herself for the battle ahead. This case would be a true test of her skills, but Rosalie Bélanger was more than ready to rise to the occasion.

Rosalie rose to her feet, her petite frame belying the commanding presence she exuded. She smoothed her tailored suit and fixed the judge with a penetrating gaze from her piercing blue eyes.

"Your Honor," she began, her voice carrying a persuasive lilt, "the prosecution's case against my client, Tom, is built on nothing more than a house of cards." She paused, allowing her words to sink in. "The evidence presented is purely circumstantial, lacking any concrete proof of Tom's involvement in this alleged counterfeit scheme."

Rosalie paced deliberately, her heels clicking on the polished floor. "We've heard a lot of speculation, Your Honor, but where's the smoking gun? Where's the irrefutable evidence linking Tom to these counterfeit bills?" She spread her hands wide, inviting the court to consider her words.

As she spoke, Rosalie noted Alessandra's subtle shift in posture, the slight narrowing of her eyes. "Good," Rosalie thought, suppressing a smirk. "She's feeling the pressure."

Alessandra stood as Rosalie concluded, her slim figure radiating determination. "Your Honor," she began, her voice clear and composed, "while my esteemed colleague speaks of speculation, we deal in facts." She gestured to the stack of files before her. "We have meticulously prepared a case that not only links the defendant to this counterfeit operation but proves his integral role beyond a shadow of a doubt."

Rosalie watched as Alessandra deftly laid out her argument, emphasizing the forensic evidence with practiced ease. "She's good," Rosalie admitted to herself, "but I'm better."

"Furthermore," Alessandra continued, her warm smile belying the steel in her words, "we have the expert testimony of Dr. François Girard, whose unparalleled expertise in paper analysis and printing techniques will demonstrate the undeniable connection between the counterfeit bills and the equipment found in the defendant's possession."

As Alessandra spoke, Rosalie's mind raced, formulating counterarguments and identifying potential weaknesses. The courtroom may have been Alessandra's stage at the moment, but Rosalie Bélanger was far from defeated. She was just getting started.

Dr. François Girard took the stand, his wiry frame settling into the witness box with a slight adjustment of his round glasses. The courtroom fell silent, all eyes fixed on the disheveled expert.

"Dr. Girard," Alessandra began, her voice warm but professional, "could you please explain to the court your findings regarding the counterfeit bills?"

Rosalie leaned forward, her piercing blue eyes locked on the witness. She watched as Dr. Girard cleared his throat, his soft voice carrying an unexpected authority.

"Certainly," he replied, his French accent adding a touch of sophistication to his words. "The counterfeit bills we examined possess a unique watermark pattern that precisely matches the custom paper found in the printing setup at Ms. Tremblay's residence."

Rosalie's mind raced, formulating her strategy. She glanced at Giselle, noting the redhead's worried expression.

Dr. Girard continued, "Furthermore, the ink composition is identical to the specialized mixture we discovered in the defendant's workshop. It's a proprietary blend, not commercially available."

As he spoke, Rosalie jotted down notes, her pen moving swiftly across the legal pad. She couldn't help but admire the doctor's expertise, even as she prepared to dismantle his testimony.

"In your professional opinion," Alessandra asked, "what is the likelihood that these counterfeits were produced using equipment other than that found in Ms. Tremblay's home?"

Dr. Girard paused, his eyes narrowing in thought. "Extremely unlikely. The combination of unique paper, ink, and printing techniques creates a forensic fingerprint, if you will. It's as distinctive as DNA."

Rosalie stood, smoothing her impeccable suit. "Your Honor, I'd like to cross-examine the witness."

As she approached Dr. Girard, Rosalie allowed a small, disarming smile to play across her lips. "Dr. Girard, your expertise is truly impressive," she began, her tone respectful yet probing. "However, I'm curious about the margin of error in your analysis. Could you elaborate on that?"

The tension in the courtroom was palpable as Alessandra Bianchi stood, her posture radiating confidence. "Your Honor, the prosecution would like to call a surprise witness."

Rosalie's eyes narrowed, her mind racing to anticipate Alessandra's next move. She watched as a wiry man in his late thirties was escorted to the stand, his nervous energy evident in the way he fidgeted with his hands.

"Please state your name for the record," Alessandra requested, her voice steady and clear.

"Marcus Dupont," the man replied, his eyes darting around the courtroom.

"Mr. Dupont, how do you know the defendant, Tom Beauchamp?"

Marcus cleared his throat. "I... I used to work with Tom at his brake pad factory."

Rosalie leaned forward, her keen gaze fixed on the witness. Something about his demeanor set off alarm bells in her head.

"And did you have any involvement with Mr. Beauchamp's recent... activities?" Alessandra pressed.

Marcus nodded, his voice dropping to almost a whisper. "Yeah, I helped him set up the printing press. He said it was for a new business venture, but I realized later what was really going on."

Tom's face paled, and Rosalie could almost hear his thoughts racing. She placed a reassuring hand on his arm as she stood. "Your Honor, I'd like to cross-examine the witness."

As Rosalie approached Marcus, her blue eyes glinted with determination. "Mr. Dupont, when exactly did you work with Mr. Beauchamp?"

"Uh, about two years ago," Marcus stammered.

Rosalie's lips curved into a slight smile. "Interesting. And yet, Mr. Beauchamp only sold his factory six months ago. Can you explain this discrepancy?"

Marcus shifted uncomfortably. "I... I might have gotten the dates mixed up."

"Mixed up by a year and a half?" Rosalie pressed, her tone skeptical. "Mr. Dupont, have you ever been convicted of a crime?"

Rosalie's relentless questioning had Marcus squirming in his seat, his credibility crumbling with each faltering response. She could feel the momentum shifting in her favor, the jury's doubtful glances at the prosecution fueling her confidence.

Just as she was about to deliver her coup de grâce, a thunderous crash echoed through the courtroom. Rosalie whirled around, her carefully styled hair whipping across her face.

A young spectator, his face flushed with embarrassment, had knocked over a large tray of exhibit papers. Documents fluttered through the air like confetti, creating a whirlwind of chaos. Jurors ducked, the bailiff rushed forward, and Alessandra scrambled to salvage what she could of her meticulous case files.

Rosalie's sharp mind clicked into overdrive. This was her chance. As the judge banged his gavel, calling for order, she raised her voice just loud enough to be heard over the commotion.

"Well," she quipped, her tone dripping with sarcasm, "it seems the prosecution's case is quite literally falling apart before our eyes."

A ripple of laughter spread through the courtroom. Even a few jurors couldn't suppress their chuckles. Rosalie caught Tom's eye, noticing the glimmer of hope that hadn't been there moments before.

She thought to herself, 'Perfect timing. Sometimes chaos is a ladder, and I intend to climb it all the way to an acquittal.'

The judge's gavel cracked through the air like a gunshot. "Order! Order in the court!" His stern voice cut through the lingering chuckles and rustling papers.

Rosalie smoothed her suit jacket, a smirk tugging at the corner of her lips. She turned back to Dr. Girard, who sat uncomfortably in the witness stand, his fingers fidgeting with his tie.

"Now, Dr. Girard," Rosalie began, her voice honey-smooth but laced with steel, "you mentioned earlier that the printing techniques used in the counterfeit bills were 'unmistakably similar' to those found in Mr. Beauchamp's home. Could you elaborate on what exactly makes them 'unmistakable'?"

As Dr. Girard launched into a technical explanation, Rosalie's mind raced. 'Time to poke some holes in this swiss cheese of a case,' she thought.

She interrupted, "So, Dr. Girard, would you say these techniques are unique to Mr. Beauchamp, or are they common in the printing industry?"

Dr. Girard hesitated, his confidence wavering. "Well, they're... they're relatively common, but-"

"Thank you, Doctor," Rosalie cut in, her smile predatory. "No further questions, Your Honor."

As she turned back to her seat, Rosalie caught sight of Alessandra's determined expression. The prosecutor was practically vibrating with barely contained energy.

"Your Honor," Alessandra said, rising to her feet, "the prosecution would like to present new evidence."

Rosalie's eyebrows shot up. 'What ace does she have up her sleeve?' she wondered, her stomach tightening with anticipation.

Alessandra's voice rang out clear and confident. "We have obtained a recorded conversation between Mr. Beauchamp and an undercover agent, clearly demonstrating his intent to sell counterfeit bills."

The courtroom erupted in murmurs. Rosalie's eyes darted to Tom, whose face had drained of all color. For the first time since the trial began, she felt a flicker of doubt.

Rosalie's mind whirred into action, her piercing blue eyes narrowing as she listened to the recording. Tom's voice, unmistakable yet somehow distant, filled the courtroom. As the last words faded, she rose to her feet, her petite frame radiating an aura of authority that belied her stature.

"Your Honor," Rosalie began, her voice crisp and controlled, "I must challenge the authenticity of this recording." She paced deliberately before the jury box, each step measured and purposeful.

"Ladies and gentlemen of the jury," she continued, her gaze sweeping across their faces, "we live in an age where technology can be manipulated with alarming ease. This recording, dramatic as it may seem, could easily have been doctored or taken entirely out of context."

Rosalie paused, allowing her words to sink in. She could feel the weight of the jury's attention, their uncertainty palpable in the air. 'Perfect,' she thought, suppressing a smile.

"Consider, if you will, the convenience of this evidence," she pressed on. "Presented at the eleventh hour, with no opportunity for proper examination or verification. Is this the foundation upon which we build justice?"

As she spoke, Rosalie's mind raced ahead, weaving together the threads of her closing argument. The chaotic paper shower from earlier, the questionable forensic evidence, the surprise witness whose credibility she'd shredded – all of it formed a tapestry of reasonable doubt.

She took a deep breath, ready to deliver the final blow. "In light of the inconsistencies we've seen today, the dubious nature of the evidence presented, and the veritable circus this trial has become," – here, she allowed a wry smile to play across her lips – "I ask you, can you truly say, beyond a reasonable doubt, that my client is guilty?"

Rosalie's words hung in the air, heavy with implication. As she returned to her seat, she caught sight of Tom's face. His expression was a mixture of hope and fear, and for a moment, Rosalie felt a twinge of... something. Doubt? Guilt? She pushed the feeling aside. 'Win first, contemplate ethics later,' she reminded herself, settling in for the judge's final instructions to the jury.

The judge's gavel cracked through the tension-filled air, causing Tom to flinch. His eyes darted from the stern-faced judge to the stoic jurors, then back to Rosalie, searching for any hint of reassurance.

"Ladies and gentlemen of the jury," the judge intoned, his voice resonating through the hushed courtroom, "you have heard all the evidence presented. It is now your duty to deliberate and reach a verdict."

As the jury began to file out, Tom leaned towards Rosalie, his voice barely above a whisper. "What do you think? Do we have a chance?"

Rosalie patted his hand, her expression carefully neutral. "We've given them plenty to think about, Tom. Now we wait."

Tom nodded, his throat tight. He watched the last juror disappear behind the heavy wooden door, feeling as though his future was walking away with them. The courtroom buzzed with muted conversation as spectators began to disperse.

'How did I end up here?' Tom thought, his mind drifting back to his modest brake pad factory, to the dreams that had seemed so attainable. 'One moment you're planning for a better life, the next you're facing years behind bars.'

As the bailiff approached to escort him back to holding, Tom cast one last glance around the courtroom. His eyes met Alessandra's, and for a fleeting second, he thought he saw a flicker of doubt cross her face. Or was it just wishful thinking?

The door closed behind him with a resounding click, leaving Tom alone with his thoughts and the unbearable weight of uncertainty.

Chapter 17

The heavy oak doors of Courtroom 12 swung open with a satisfying creak as Rosalie Bélanger strode in, her heels clicking decisively on the polished floor. She adjusted her crisp navy blazer, feeling the comforting weight of the files tucked inside. A wry smile played at the corners of her mouth as she caught sight of the prosecution team huddled near the front, looking about as cheerful as a group of wet cats.

Rosalie's eyes narrowed as she zeroed in on her targets: Agent Alessandra Bianchi and Dr. François Girard. Time to work some legal magic.

"Good morning, counselors," Rosalie purred, approaching the group with feline grace. "Lovely day for a little negotiation, wouldn't you agree?"

Agent Bianchi's spine stiffened visibly. "Ms. Bélanger," she acknowledged coolly. "I wasn't aware we had anything left to discuss."

Rosalie's smile widened. Oh, if they only knew what she had up her sleeve. She glanced at Dr. Girard, who was absently cleaning his glasses, looking as if he'd rather be anywhere else.

"On the contrary, Agent Bianchi," Rosalie countered, her voice smooth as silk. "I believe we have a matter of utmost importance to discuss. One that could significantly impact the outcome of this case."

She paused dramatically, savoring the moment. The air in the courtroom seemed to crackle with tension.

Dr. Girard finally looked up, curiosity piqued. "What exactly are you proposing, Ms. Bélanger?"

Rosalie leaned in conspiratorially, her voice dropping to a stage whisper. "Let's just say I have information that could be... mutually beneficial. But first, we need to establish some ground rules."

As she spoke, Rosalie's mind raced, calculating every possible outcome. This was her element – the thrill of the courtroom, the dance of negotiation. She lived for moments like these.

Agent Bianchi crossed her arms, skepticism etched on her face. "We're listening, counselor. But I hope for your sake this isn't another one of your infamous wild goose chases."

Rosalie chuckled, a rich, warm sound that belied the steel beneath. "Oh, Agent Bianchi, you wound me. When have I ever led you astray?" She winked, knowing full well the answer to that question.

As she prepared to lay out her offer, Rosalie felt a surge of adrenaline. This was it – her final play, her ace in the hole. And if she played her cards right, she just might pull off the impossible.

Rosalie straightened her posture, her piercing blue eyes scanning the faces of the prosecution team. She took a deep breath, savoring the moment before diving in.

"Ladies and gentlemen," she began, her voice steady and authoritative, "we have a unique opportunity before us. My client is prepared to assist in the recovery of $200 million in counterfeit currency."

Agent Bianchi's eyebrows shot up, but Rosalie continued before she could interject. "Now, I don't need to remind you of the catastrophic impact this amount of fake cash could have on our economy if it were to circulate. We're talking about potential destabilization of the U.S. dollar."

Dr. Girard leaned forward, his interest clearly piqued. "And your client can lead us to this money?"

Rosalie allowed herself a small, triumphant smile. "Precisely, Doctor. But of course, such cooperation would need to be met with... shall we say, a degree of leniency?"

Agent Bianchi scoffed, but Rosalie could see the wheels turning behind her eyes. The agent glanced at her colleagues, a silent conversation passing between them.

After what felt like an eternity, but was likely only a few seconds, Agent Bianchi spoke. "We'll need more than just your word, Ms.

Bélanger. Concrete proof of the money's location would be required before we even consider any kind of deal."

Rosalie nodded, having anticipated this response. "Of course, Agent. I wouldn't expect anything less from the illustrious U.S. Secret Service."

As she prepared her next move, Rosalie felt a familiar thrill coursing through her veins. This was the moment that would make or break her case, and she was determined to come out on top.

Tom's heart raced as he watched the exchange between Rosalie and the prosecutors. The tension in the room was palpable, thick enough to cut with a knife. He knew this was his moment. Taking a deep breath, Tom stepped forward, his eyes fixed on Agent Bianchi.

"I'll do it," he declared, his voice steady despite the nervous energy coursing through him. "I'll lead you to the money myself."

The room fell silent. Tom could feel all eyes on him, scrutinizing his every move. He straightened his shoulders, determined to project confidence.

Rosalie turned to him, a mix of surprise and approval in her piercing blue eyes. "Mr. Beauchamp, are you certain?"

Tom nodded, his resolve strengthening. "Absolutely. It's time to make this right."

Agent Bianchi raised an eyebrow. "And we're supposed to trust you just like that?"

"You don't have to trust me," Tom replied, a hint of his old businessman swagger creeping into his voice. "But I'm your best shot at finding that money before it hits the streets."

Rosalie cleared her throat. "If I may, I'd like a moment to confer with my client."

As the prosecutors nodded their assent, Rosalie guided Tom to a corner of the room. The familiar scent of her perfume – a mix of jasmine and something crisp he couldn't quite place – filled his nostrils.

"Tom," she whispered, her tone urgent but controlled. "Are you absolutely sure about this? Once we commit, there's no turning back."

He met her gaze, seeing the concern behind her professional facade. "I'm sure, Rosalie. It's the only way out of this mess."

She nodded, her mind already racing ahead. "Alright, then we need to plan this carefully. Where exactly is the money?"

Tom leaned in closer, his voice barely audible. "It's in a box truck. Parked at the Sunset Inn, just off the highway."

Rosalie's eyes widened slightly. "Clever. Hiding in plain sight." She paused, considering. "We'll need to be careful about how we approach this. Any unexpected moves could spook potential accomplices or put us at risk."

Tom felt a flutter of anxiety in his stomach. "What do you suggest?"

"We'll request a small team," Rosalie murmured, her eyes darting to the prosecutors across the room. "Emphasize the need for discretion. We don't want to attract attention and risk losing the money."

Tom nodded, impressed once again by Rosalie's quick thinking. "And once we get there?"

"You'll lead them to the truck," she said firmly. "But let me do the talking if anyone questions us. Remember, every word can be used against you."

As they turned back to face the prosecutors, Tom felt a mix of dread and determination. This was it – his last chance at redemption. He just hoped it wouldn't blow up in his face.

Tom's shoes squeaked on the polished courthouse floor as he and Rosalie made their way towards the exit, flanked by a small group of stern-faced officers. The weight of the moment pressed down on him, making each step feel like a monumental effort.

"Remember," Rosalie whispered, her breath warm against his ear, "stay calm and follow my lead."

Tom nodded, swallowing hard. "Got it. Cool as a cucumber, that's me."

As they stepped out into the late afternoon sun, Tom squinted, his eyes adjusting to the brightness. A convoy of unmarked vehicles waited for them, engines humming quietly.

"Nice and discreet," Tom muttered, a nervous chuckle escaping his lips.

Rosalie shot him a warning glance. "Focus, Tom. This is crucial."

They climbed into the lead car, an officer sliding in beside them. As the convoy pulled away from the curb, Tom's heart began to race. He wiped his sweaty palms on his trousers, trying to steady his breathing.

"Take a left here," Tom instructed the driver, his voice cracking slightly. He cleared his throat. "Then straight for about three miles."

As they drove, the cityscape gave way to suburbia, then to a more industrial area. Tom's mind raced, replaying every detail of his plan, searching for any overlooked flaws.

"We're almost there," he said, more to himself than anyone else. "Just past this intersection, then..."

The Sunset Inn came into view, its faded sign a beacon of both hope and anxiety for Tom. He pointed to the entrance. "Pull in here. The truck's parked around back."

As the convoy turned into the parking lot, Tom's heart pounded so loudly he was sure everyone could hear it. This was it – the moment of truth.

As the vehicles rolled to a stop in the nearly empty parking lot, Tom's senses went into overdrive. The air felt thick with tension, and every sound seemed amplified – the crunch of gravel under tires, the ping of cooling engines, even his own shallow breathing.

Tom scanned the area, his eyes darting from one corner to another. A lone shopping cart rattled in the breeze, and a stray dog sniffed around a dumpster. Everything else was still.

"Looks clear," he murmured, more to calm himself than inform the others.

An officer beside him shifted, hand resting on his holster. "Where's the truck, Mr. Beauchamp?"

Tom took a deep breath, steadying himself. "Right over there," he said, pointing to a nondescript box truck parked near the hotel's service entrance. "The white one with the faded logo."

As they approached the vehicle, Tom's mind raced. 'This is it,' he thought. 'No turning back now. Just stay calm and see it through.'

He turned to the group of officers, his voice low but firm. "The money's in the back, hidden among some ordinary moving boxes. It's... it's a lot to take in."

Tom fumbled with the keys, his hands shaking slightly as he unlocked the truck's rear door. He paused, hand on the latch, and looked at the expectant faces around him.

"I know this doesn't make up for what I've done," he said, his tone tinged with regret and determination. "But I hope it's a start."

With that, Tom lifted the latch and swung the door open, revealing stacks of cardboard boxes. To the untrained eye, it looked like nothing more than abandoned furniture and knick-knacks.

"It's all here," Tom said, gesturing to the seemingly innocent cargo. "Two hundred million in counterfeit bills, hidden in plain sight."

The officers exchanged glances before one of them, a stern-faced man with salt-and-pepper hair, stepped forward. "Alright, let's get to work," he ordered, pulling on a pair of latex gloves.

Tom watched as the team methodically began their inspection, opening boxes and rifling through their contents. The air was thick with tension, broken only by the occasional rustle of paper or murmured conversation.

"My God," one of the younger officers breathed, holding up a stack of bills. "These look... real."

Tom couldn't help but feel a twinge of pride, quickly followed by shame. "They should," he said quietly. "We put a lot of work into making them as authentic as possible."

The lead officer turned to Tom, his expression unreadable. "You realize the gravity of what you've done here, don't you, Mr. Beauchamp?"

Tom nodded, his throat tight. "I do. That's why I'm here now, trying to make it right."

As the inspection continued, Tom's mind wandered to the events that had led him to this moment. The long nights, the careful planning, the thrill of success... and the crushing weight of guilt that followed.

Finally, after what felt like hours, the lead officer approached Tom. "Well, Mr. Beauchamp, it seems you weren't lying. It's all here, just as you said."

Tom let out a breath he didn't realize he'd been holding. "So, what happens now?" he asked, his voice barely above a whisper.

The officer's face softened slightly. "Now, we secure the money and head back. You've done the right thing here, even if it took you a while to get there."

As the last of the counterfeit bills were loaded into secure containers, Tom felt a wave of relief wash over him. He'd done it. He'd faced his mistakes and taken the first step towards redemption.

The courthouse doors swung open as Rosalie strode in, her heels clicking purposefully on the polished floor. Tom followed close behind, his shoulders squared with newfound resolve. The prosecution team awaited them, their faces a mix of curiosity and skepticism.

Rosalie approached the table, a confident smile playing on her lips. "Gentlemen, lady," she nodded to Agent Bianchi, "I believe we have some business to conclude."

Tom's heart raced as he watched Rosalie lay out the evidence – photographs, GPS coordinates, and a detailed inventory of the recovered counterfeit money. His mind drifted to the weight that had been lifted from his shoulders. 'It's almost over,' he thought, a glimmer of hope sparking in his chest.

"As you can see," Rosalie continued, her voice steady and persuasive, "my client has fully cooperated and delivered on his promise. The threat to our economy has been neutralized."

The lead prosecutor, a stern-faced man in his fifties, leaned forward. "And what exactly are you proposing in return, Ms. Bélanger?"

Tom held his breath, his future hanging on Rosalie's next words.

"Given Mr. Beauchamp's unprecedented cooperation and the service he's rendered to this country, we're seeking a significantly reduced sentence. Time served, plus five years probation."

The room fell silent. Tom's eyes darted between the prosecutors, trying to read their expressions. The tension was palpable.

Finally, Agent Bianchi spoke up. "It's a fair offer. Without Mr. Beauchamp's assistance, we might never have recovered that money."

After what felt like an eternity, the lead prosecutor nodded. "We'll agree to your terms, Ms. Bélanger. Mr. Beauchamp, you're a very lucky man."

Relief flooded through Tom's body. He turned to Rosalie, a mix of gratitude and disbelief in his eyes. "We did it," he whispered.

Rosalie's usually stern face softened into a genuine smile. "We certainly did, Tom. It's been quite a journey, hasn't it?"

As they exited the courthouse, Tom paused on the steps, taking in the warmth of the sun on his face. "I never thought I'd see this day," he mused, his voice tinged with wonder.

Rosalie chuckled beside him. "That's the thing about life, Tom. It's full of surprises – some good, some bad. What matters is how we handle them."

Tom nodded, a wry smile crossing his face. "Well, I'd say we handled this one pretty well, wouldn't you?"

They shared a laugh, the sound of their voices carrying on the breeze – a fitting end to their improbable adventure.

Chapter 18

The heavy oak doors of Courtroom 3 creaked open, and Tom Beauchamp felt his heart hammering against his ribs. He tugged at his navy tie, suddenly feeling like it was choking him. Beside him, Rosalie Bélanger strode confidently into the room, her sharp black heels clicking against the polished floor.

"Deep breaths, Tom," Rosalie murmured, giving his arm a reassuring squeeze. "We've prepared for this."

Tom nodded, trying to swallow the lump in his throat. As they made their way to the defense table, he couldn't help but notice the sea of faces turned towards him - some curious, some judgmental. The weight of their stares made his palms sweat.

'This is it,' he thought, his mind racing. 'Everything I've worked for comes down to this moment.'

As they took their seats, Tom's eyes darted to the prosecution table. Agent Alessandra Bianchi sat there, cool and composed in her crisp white blouse. Beside her, Dr. François Girard fiddled with his glasses, a stack of papers neatly arranged before him.

The judge entered, and everyone rose. Tom's legs felt like jelly as he stood.

"Be seated," the judge intoned, and the rustle of movement filled the room.

Agent Bianchi rose gracefully, her voice clear and authoritative as she addressed the court. "Your Honor, the prosecution will demonstrate that Mr. Beauchamp orchestrated a counterfeit scheme of unprecedented scale and sophistication."

Tom's stomach churned. He leaned towards Rosalie, whispering, "They make it sound so... calculated."

Rosalie patted his hand. "Let them talk. We'll have our turn."

As Agent Bianchi continued outlining the case, Tom found his gaze drawn to Dr. Girard. The scientist was nodding along, occasionally pushing his glasses up his nose with a bony finger.

'He looks more like an absent-minded professor than a forensic expert,' Tom mused, a hint of a smile tugging at his lips despite the gravity of the situation.

His amusement was short-lived as Agent Bianchi's words cut through his thoughts. "...potential to destabilize entire economies. Mr. Beauchamp's actions posed a very real threat to the global financial system."

Tom felt the blood drain from his face. He hadn't thought of it in those terms before. As the prosecution painted a picture of the far-reaching consequences of his actions, he found himself wondering, 'Was I really capable of all that?'

The gravity of the situation settled over him like a heavy blanket. As he listened to the damning evidence being presented, Tom realized that this courtroom drama was far from the triumphant finale he had imagined for his audacious plan. Instead, it was the moment of reckoning, where the true weight of his actions would finally be measured.

Rosalie stood up, her petite frame belying the force of her presence. "Your Honor," she began, her voice clear and authoritative, "while the prosecution paints a dramatic picture, we must focus on the facts of this case, not hypothetical scenarios."

Tom watched, his heart racing, as Rosalie moved towards the center of the courtroom. She exuded confidence, and for a moment, he allowed himself to hope.

"Let's examine the surveillance footage," Rosalie continued, gesturing towards a screen. "At first glance, it may seem incriminating, but upon closer inspection..." She paused for effect, her blue eyes scanning the courtroom. "The timestamp clearly shows a discrepancy of three minutes between the alleged transaction and Mr. Beauchamp's presence on the premises."

Tom leaned forward, his brow furrowed. He hadn't noticed that detail before. As Rosalie dissected the evidence, pointing out inconsistencies and gaps, he felt a glimmer of optimism.

Suddenly, a loud screech pierced the air. Everyone winced as Rosalie's microphone emitted an ear-splitting feedback.

"My apologies," Rosalie said, tapping the mic. "As I was saying—"

Another screech. Tom couldn't help but chuckle as Rosalie's composed facade cracked slightly, a flash of irritation crossing her face.

Just then, the bailiff rushed forward to assist, tripping over his own feet and stumbling into a chair. The chair skidded across the floor with a loud screech, creating a cacophony that rivaled the malfunctioning microphone.

As chaos erupted in the courtroom, Tom thought to himself, 'Is this really happening? It's like something out of a sitcom.'

Despite the absurdity of the situation, he couldn't shake the nagging worry. Would these technical difficulties derail Rosalie's carefully constructed defense?

Rosalie cleared her throat, regaining her composure as the courtroom settled. She stepped away from the faulty microphone, her voice projecting clearly without it.

"Your Honor," she began, her tone passionate yet controlled, "my client, Mr. Beauchamp, has demonstrated exceptional cooperation throughout this investigation. He has willingly provided crucial information that will lead authorities to recover $200 million in counterfeit currency."

Tom's heart raced as he watched Rosalie, her petite frame commanding the room. He marveled at her ability to weave a compelling narrative from the threads of his mistakes.

"This cooperation," Rosalie continued, her blue eyes intense, "speaks volumes about Mr. Beauchamp's character and his genuine remorse. He's not just a man who made a grave error in judgment, but one who's actively working to right his wrongs."

Tom felt a lump form in his throat. He hadn't realized how much he'd changed until hearing it laid out so eloquently.

"Your Honor, I implore you to consider the broader implications of Mr. Beauchamp's actions. His assistance will prevent potential economic destabilization and protect countless innocent citizens."

As Rosalie concluded her impassioned plea, the judge leaned back, his expression unreadable. The courtroom fell into a tense silence.

Tom's palms grew sweaty as he waited. He thought, 'This is it. Everything hinges on what happens next.' The weight of the moment pressed down on him, making each second feel like an eternity.

The judge leaned forward, his gavel poised. The sharp crack echoed through the courtroom, causing Tom to flinch. He held his breath, his heart pounding so loudly he was sure everyone could hear it.

"Mr. Beauchamp," the judge began, his voice firm yet not unkind, "after careful consideration of the evidence presented and your cooperation with the authorities, I have decided to accept the terms of your deal."

Tom's eyes widened, a spark of hope igniting in his chest. He glanced at Rosalie, who gave him a subtle nod.

The judge continued, "In exchange for the location of the remaining counterfeit money, you will be granted a lenient sentence of community service and probation. You are to assist the Secret Service in their ongoing investigation and education efforts regarding counterfeit currency."

A wave of relief washed over Tom. He exhaled slowly, trying to process the judge's words. 'Community service? Probation? I'm... free?'

"Thank you, Your Honor," Tom managed to say, his voice slightly hoarse with emotion. "I promise to make the most of this opportunity."

As the reality of the situation sank in, a smile spread across Tom's face. He couldn't help but marvel at the unexpected turn of events.

'All those sleepless nights, the meticulous planning, the constant fear of discovery... and here I am, walking away a free man.'

Tom turned to Rosalie, his eyes brimming with gratitude. "I don't know how to thank you," he whispered.

She smiled back, her professional demeanor softening slightly. "Just keep your promise, Tom. Make it count."

Tom's gaze locked with Rosalie's, a current of shared triumph passing between them. Her usually stern blue eyes sparkled with a hint of pride, and the corner of her mouth twitched upward in a barely perceptible smile.

"We did it," Tom mouthed silently, his chest swelling with a mixture of relief and admiration for his tenacious lawyer.

Rosalie gave a subtle nod, her perfectly coiffed dark hair catching the light. "You're welcome," she whispered back, her voice carrying a warmth that Tom had rarely heard from her.

As they gathered their belongings, Tom's mind raced. 'I can't believe it's over. All those nights of planning, the constant fear... and now, freedom.'

They made their way out of the courtroom, Tom's legs feeling slightly wobbly as the adrenaline began to subside. The corridor seemed brighter somehow, as if the weight of uncertainty had been lifted from his shoulders.

Pushing through the heavy wooden doors, Tom stepped outside, blinking in the sunlight. Before he could fully adjust to the brightness, a familiar figure came rushing towards him.

"Tom!" Giselle's voice rang out, filled with a mixture of joy and relief.

He barely had time to react before she threw her arms around him, pulling him into a tight embrace. Tom breathed in the familiar scent of her perfume, feeling the tension in his body melt away.

"You're free," Giselle whispered, her voice thick with emotion. "I was so worried, but you did it."

Tom pulled back slightly, taking in her flushed cheeks and the unshed tears glistening in her green eyes. "We did it," he corrected gently, thinking of her unwavering support throughout the ordeal. "I couldn't have done this without you, Giselle."

As Tom and Giselle savored their reunion, the scene around them dissolved into a whirlwind of activity. The courthouse steps became a stage for a comedic montage of loose ends being frantically tied up.

Sergeant Jean-Guy Tremblay's gruff voice echoed through the police station. "Tabarnac! This paperwork is worse than a bowl of poutine left out overnight!" He furiously shuffled through a mountain of documents, his salt-and-pepper hair standing on end from running his hands through it in frustration.

Meanwhile, across town, Patrice Dubois, the once-imposing figure, was comically hunched over a paper shredder in his opulent office. "Merde," he muttered, shoving stacks of counterfeit bills into the machine. The shredder groaned in protest, billowing smoke as it struggled to keep up with Patrice's frantic pace.

Tom chuckled to himself, imagining the chaos unfolding. "I wonder how everyone else is faring," he mused aloud.

Giselle raised an eyebrow, a mischievous glint in her eye. "Well, I heard through the grapevine that your old employee, François from the brake pad factory, has opened a bakery."

"François? A baker?" Tom's eyes widened in disbelief. "The man who couldn't even operate a coffee machine without setting off the fire alarm?"

As if on cue, a plume of smoke rose from a nearby storefront, followed by the shrill wail of a fire alarm. François emerged, covered in flour and looking sheepish.

"Some things never change," Giselle giggled, her Quebecois accent more pronounced in her amusement.

Tom shook his head, a mixture of fondness and exasperation coloring his features. "At least he's found his passion, even if it comes with a side of char."

Tom and Giselle strolled hand in hand through the bustling streets of Montreal, their laughter mingling with the ambient sounds of the city. The weight of their past adventures had lifted, replaced by a lightness that seemed to quicken their steps.

"You know, Giselle," Tom mused, his eyes crinkling at the corners, "I never thought I'd say this, but I'm actually looking forward to a quiet evening at home."

Giselle's green eyes sparkled with amusement. "Really? The great Tom Beauchamp, mastermind extraordinaire, craving domesticity?"

Tom chuckled, running a hand through his graying hair. "What can I say? You've domesticated me."

They paused at a small park, settling onto a bench. Tom watched a group of children playing, their carefree laughter stirring something within him.

"It's funny," he said softly, "how the simple things suddenly mean so much more."

Giselle leaned her head on his shoulder, her fiery red hair catching the late afternoon sun. "Like what?"

"Like this," Tom gestured around them. "Just sitting here, watching the world go by. No schemes, no pressure. Just... living."

Giselle intertwined her fingers with his, her voice taking on a teasing tone. "Are you getting soft on me, mon chéri?"

Tom's eyes twinkled mischievously. "Never. In fact," he leaned in closer, lowering his voice conspiratorially, "I was thinking... maybe we could plan a little trip?"

Giselle sat up straight, her curiosity piqued. "Oh? And where might this trip take us?"

"I hear Monaco is lovely this time of year," Tom said, a familiar glint of excitement in his eyes.

Giselle's laughter rang out, drawing curious glances from passersby. "Tom Beauchamp, you incorrigible man! Are you suggesting what I think you're suggesting?"

Tom's grin widened. "I'm just saying, we've got some skills that shouldn't go to waste. And think of the thrill!"

As they stood to leave, their eyes met, a silent understanding passing between them. The future stretched out before them, full of possibility and adventure.

"Well," Giselle said, her voice warm with affection and a hint of excitement, "I suppose life would be awfully dull without a little... excitement now and then."

Tom chuckled, wrapping an arm around Giselle's waist as they strolled along the sun-dappled path. The crisp autumn air carried the scent of fallen leaves and distant woodsmoke.

"Dull is the last thing I'd ever want for us," he said, his voice low and warm. "But maybe we should start small. You know, ease back into things."

Giselle raised an eyebrow, a smirk playing at her lips. "Oh? And what did you have in mind, mon amour?"

Tom's eyes sparkled with mischief. "Well, I heard the local art museum is getting a new exhibit next month. Priceless sculptures, I believe."

"Tom!" Giselle gasped, playfully swatting his arm. "You can't be serious!"

He laughed, holding up his hands in mock surrender. "Relax, I'm kidding. Mostly."

As they reached a small pond, Tom paused, his expression growing thoughtful. "You know, all joking aside, I really am grateful for this second chance. With you, with life."

Giselle's features softened, and she reached up to cup his cheek. "As am I, mon chéri. As am I."

They stood there for a moment, the setting sun painting the sky in brilliant hues of orange and pink. Tom felt a sense of peace wash over him, mingled with the tingling excitement of endless possibilities.

"So," he said finally, a grin tugging at his lips. "About that trip to Monaco..."

Chapter 19

The fluorescent lights of the Quebec City Jean Lesage International Airport buzzed overhead as Tom Beauchamp stepped off the jet bridge, his worn leather briefcase clutched tightly in his hand. The familiar scent of jet fuel and disinfectant filled his nostrils, a stark contrast to the crisp autumn air that awaited him outside.

Tom's heart raced as he made his way through the terminal, his eyes darting from sign to sign. "Where's the exit?" he muttered, adjusting the strap of his bag. "I swear they change this place every time I visit."

As he navigated the crowded corridors, Tom's mind wandered to Giselle. Would she be happy to see him? Or would the weight of their recent escapades have taken its toll on her usually cheerful demeanor?

Finally reaching the sliding doors, Tom stepped out into the chilly Quebec air. He took a deep breath, savoring the moment. "Well, old boy," he said to himself, "no turning back now."

Tom raised his hand, flagging down a nearby taxi. The yellow cab pulled up, and Tom climbed in, his joints creaking in protest.

"Bonjour," the driver greeted him with a thick Quebecois accent.

"Bonjour," Tom replied, his own accent betraying his non-native status. He fumbled in his pocket for the slip of paper with Giselle's address. "Can you take me to this address, please?"

The driver nodded, punching the address into his GPS. As they pulled away from the curb, Tom's gaze drifted to the passing scenery. The familiar sights of Quebec City brought a mix of comfort and apprehension.

"First time in Quebec?" the driver asked, breaking the silence.

Tom chuckled. "No, not at all. I've been here many times. But it feels different this time."

"Ah, visiting someone special?"

Tom nodded, a small smile playing on his lips. "You could say that. Someone very special indeed."

As the taxi wound its way through the city streets, Tom's fingers drummed nervously on his knee. He couldn't help but wonder what awaited him at the end of this journey. Would Giselle's fiery red hair still shine with the same vibrancy? Would her green eyes light up when she saw him, or would they be clouded with worry?

The minutes ticked by, each one feeling longer than the last. Tom's heart pounded in his chest, a steady rhythm that seemed to echo the ticking of his watch. He closed his eyes, trying to steady his breathing.

"Almost there," the driver announced, jolting Tom from his reverie.

Tom nodded, his throat suddenly dry. As they turned onto Giselle's street, he felt a mix of excitement and terror wash over him. This was it. The moment of truth.

The taxi slowed to a stop, and Tom reached for his wallet with trembling hands. "Keep the change," he said, handing over a few bills.

As he stepped out of the car, Tom took a deep breath of the crisp Quebec air. He stood there for a moment, gathering his courage, before taking his first step towards Giselle's front door.

Tom's shoes scuffed softly against the concrete as he approached Giselle's doorstep. His hand hovered over the doorbell, trembling slightly. He took a deep breath, steadying himself.

"You can do this, Tom," he muttered under his breath. "It's just Giselle."

But it wasn't just Giselle, was it? It was everything they'd been through, every lesson learned, every moment apart that had felt like an eternity. Tom's finger pressed the doorbell, and the cheerful chime seemed to echo in his ears.

As he waited, his mind raced. What if she'd changed her mind? What if-

The door swung open, and there she was. Giselle's vibrant red hair framed her face, those captivating green eyes widening in surprise and then crinkling with joy. "Tom?" she breathed, her voice carrying that familiar melodic accent.

"Giselle," Tom managed, his voice thick with emotion.

In an instant, they were in each other's arms. Tom buried his face in Giselle's hair, inhaling the familiar scent of her shampoo. He felt her arms tighten around him, her small frame pressed against his.

"I can't believe you're here," Giselle whispered, her voice muffled against his chest.

Tom chuckled softly, feeling the weight of the world lift from his shoulders. "Neither can I, to be honest. I've missed you so much, Giselle."

They pulled apart slightly, both wiping away tears. Giselle's hand cupped Tom's cheek, her thumb tracing the lines that seemed to have deepened since they'd last seen each other.

"You look... tired," she said, a hint of concern in her voice.

Tom nodded, placing his hand over hers. "It's been a long journey, in more ways than one. But I'm here now, and that's what matters."

Tom followed Giselle inside, his eyes sweeping over the familiar surroundings of her cozy apartment. Sunlight streamed through the lace curtains, casting intricate patterns on the hardwood floor. The scent of freshly brewed coffee wafted through the air, mingling with the faint aroma of Giselle's favorite lavender candles.

"I can't believe how much I've missed this place," Tom said, his voice thick with nostalgia.

Giselle's laughter, light and musical, filled the room. "Well, it's missed you too. Come on, sit down. I want to hear everything."

As they settled onto the plush sofa, Tom couldn't help but marvel at how easily they fell back into their old rhythms. Giselle curled her legs beneath her, cradling a steaming mug of coffee in her hands.

"So, Mr. Beauchamp," she began, her green eyes twinkling with mischief, "what adventures have you been up to?"

Tom chuckled, running a hand through his graying hair. "Oh, where do I even begin? Let's just say I've learned more about international shipping laws than I ever thought possible."

As they exchanged stories, Tom found himself captivated by the way Giselle's hands moved animatedly as she spoke, her accent becoming more pronounced with excitement. He realized how much he'd missed these small details.

"You know," Tom said, his tone growing serious, "being away... it's made me think a lot about what really matters."

Giselle nodded, her expression softening. "I know what you mean. It's funny how sometimes you need to step away from everything to see it clearly."

Tom took a sip of his coffee, savoring the rich flavor. "I've been thinking about consequences, Giselle. About the impact our choices have, not just on us, but on everyone around us."

"And what have you concluded?" Giselle asked, leaning forward slightly.

"That sometimes, the simplest joys are the most valuable," Tom replied, his eyes meeting hers. "And that staying true to our values... it's not always easy, but it's always worth it."

Giselle's lips curled into a mischievous smile as she set down her coffee mug. "Speaking of consequences, Tom, do you remember that time in Montreal when you tried to sweet-talk your way past customs?"

Tom groaned, but couldn't help the grin spreading across his face. "Oh God, how could I forget? I thought my 'maple syrup connoisseur' act was foolproof."

"Foolproof? Ha!" Giselle burst into laughter, her red hair shaking with each chuckle. "You should have seen your face when that agent asked you to name five maple syrup grades!"

Tom felt his cheeks flush with embarrassment, but joined in the laughter. "I panicked! I started making up names like 'Ultra-Premium Platinum' and 'Lumberjack's Delight.'"

Giselle wiped a tear from her eye, still giggling. "And then you tried to demonstrate your 'expert tasting technique'..."

"...by chugging an entire bottle of syrup," Tom finished, shaking his head. "I thought I was going to be sick for days."

As their laughter subsided, Tom's expression grew serious. He reached across the table, taking Giselle's hand in his. "You know, Giselle, I couldn't have made it through all this without you."

Giselle's green eyes softened, meeting his gaze. "Tom..."

"I mean it," he continued, his voice thick with emotion. "Your support, your loyalty... it's meant everything to me. Even when things got tough, you never wavered."

Tom squeezed Giselle's hand, his eyes crinkling at the corners as he smiled. "So, what's next for us, mon chéri? I think we've had enough excitement to last a lifetime."

Giselle leaned back in her chair, a thoughtful expression crossing her face. "Well, I've been thinking... maybe it's time we focus on building something together. Something legitimate."

"I like the sound of that," Tom nodded, his tone measured but tinged with excitement. "What did you have in mind?"

"Remember that little bookshop we always talked about? The one with the cozy reading nook and the espresso bar?" Giselle's eyes sparkled with enthusiasm.

Tom chuckled, running a hand through his graying hair. "How could I forget? It was our go-to daydream during those long stakeouts."

"Well, why not make it a reality?" Giselle leaned forward, her voice low and intense. "We could start small, build it up slowly. No more get-rich-quick schemes, no more looking over our shoulders. Just books, coffee, and peace of mind."

Tom felt a warmth spread through his chest. It was a simple dream, but after everything they'd been through, it sounded like paradise. "You know what? I think that's exactly what we need."

Suddenly, Tom remembered something. "Oh! Speaking of new beginnings, I have something for you." He reached into his pocket, pulling out a small, wrapped package.

Giselle's eyebrows shot up in surprise. "Tom, you shouldn't have!"

"It's nothing fancy," he said, sliding the gift across the table. "Just a little something I picked up during my travels. A reminder of everything we've been through together."

With delicate fingers, Giselle unwrapped the package, revealing a beautiful, hand-carved wooden maple leaf. Her breath caught in her throat as she traced the intricate details.

"Oh, Tom," she whispered, her eyes glistening. "It's beautiful."

"I saw it in a little shop in Vermont," Tom explained, his voice soft. "It made me think of you, of us. Our Canadian adventure, the sweet and the sticky parts."

Giselle laughed, a sound that warmed Tom's heart. "It's perfect. Thank you."

As they gazed at each other across the table, Tom felt a surge of gratitude for the woman before him. They'd weathered storms together, faced challenges that would have broken lesser partnerships. Yet here they were, stronger than ever, ready to build a new life.

"To our future bookshop," Tom said, raising his coffee mug in a toast.

Giselle clinked her mug against his, her smile radiant. "To our future, period."

Tom stood up, his joints creaking slightly as he stretched. "How about we take a walk? I've missed these streets more than I realized."

Giselle's eyes lit up. "That sounds perfect. Let me grab a sweater."

As they stepped out into the crisp Quebec air, Tom inhaled deeply, savoring the familiar scents of his hometown. The cobblestone streets echoed with their footsteps, and the quaint storefronts brought a smile to his face.

"You know," Tom mused, his hand intertwined with Giselle's, "I never thought I'd be so happy to see Monsieur Dubois's crooked 'Open' sign."

Giselle chuckled. "It's the little things, isn't it?"

They strolled past the local bakery, its warm, yeasty aroma wafting out onto the street. Tom's stomach growled audibly, eliciting a laugh from Giselle.

"Some things never change," she teased, nudging him playfully.

As they rounded the corner, a booming voice called out, "Well, if it isn't the prodigal son himself!"

Tom turned to see Henri, his old high school buddy, waving enthusiastically from across the street. Henri jogged over, enveloping Tom in a bear hug that nearly knocked the wind out of him.

"Easy there, big guy," Tom wheezed, patting Henri's back. "I'd like to keep my ribs intact."

Henri stepped back, grinning from ear to ear. "Tom, my friend, it's good to have you back. We were starting to think you'd found greener pastures."

Tom's mind flashed to the events of the past few months – the schemes, the close calls, the lessons learned. He chuckled wryly. "Trust me, Henri, there's no place like home."

As they chatted, Tom couldn't help but marvel at the simple joy of catching up with an old friend. It was a far cry from the high-stakes situations he'd found himself in recently, and he relished every moment of it.

The conversation with Henri eventually wound down, and Tom and Giselle found themselves drawn to the cheerful sounds emanating from the nearby park. As they approached, the sight of children playing on the swings and slides brought a smile to both their faces.

Tom gestured to an empty bench. "Shall we?"

Giselle nodded, her green eyes twinkling. "I thought you'd never ask."

They settled onto the worn wooden seat, their shoulders touching. Tom watched a young boy struggle to climb the jungle gym, his tiny face scrunched in determination.

"Remember when life was that simple?" Tom mused, his voice tinged with nostalgia. "When your biggest worry was conquering the monkey bars?"

Giselle leaned her head on his shoulder. "Oui, those were the days. No elaborate schemes, no international intrigue..."

Tom winced slightly. "Point taken. But you have to admit, it wasn't all bad, was it?"

"Non, not all bad," Giselle conceded with a soft laugh. "But I prefer this – us, here, now."

As the sun began its descent, painting the sky in hues of orange and pink, Tom stood and offered his hand to Giselle. "Ready to head home?"

She took it, intertwining her fingers with his. "Lead the way, mon amour."

They walked hand in hand, the cooling evening air nipping at their cheeks. Tom's mind raced with possibilities for their future, each step bringing them closer to their shared dreams.

As they reached their front door, Tom paused, key in hand. "Giselle, I just want you to know... I'm ready for our fresh start. Whatever comes next, we'll face it together."

Giselle's smile was radiant as she squeezed his hand. "Together," she echoed, as they stepped inside, ready to embrace their new beginning.

Tom and Giselle moved to the living room window, drawn by the breathtaking sunset painting the sky in vibrant hues of orange, pink, and purple. They stood side by side, their silhouettes framed by the fading light.

"It's beautiful, isn't it?" Tom murmured, his eyes fixed on the horizon. He felt a sense of peace wash over him, a stark contrast to the tumultuous journey that had led them here.

Giselle nodded, her red hair catching the last rays of sunlight. "Oui, it is. I never thought I'd appreciate something as simple as a sunset so much."

Tom chuckled softly, his gaze shifting to her. "You know, all those elaborate plans I made, all the risks we took... and here we are, finding joy in this moment."

"Life has a funny way of teaching us lessons, non?" Giselle replied, a hint of amusement in her voice.

As they watched the sun dip lower, Tom's mind wandered to all they'd been through. The schemes, the close calls, the moments of doubt and fear. Yet somehow, they'd made it through stronger than ever.

"I couldn't have done any of it without you, Giselle," Tom said, his voice thick with emotion. "Your loyalty, your quick thinking... you've been my rock through all of this."

Giselle turned to face him, her green eyes sparkling with unshed tears. "And you, Tom, have shown me what it means to dream big, to take risks for what you believe in."

They shared a knowing smile, years of shared experiences passing between them in that single look. As the last sliver of sun disappeared below the horizon, Tom wrapped an arm around Giselle's waist, pulling her close.

"So, what's next for us?" he asked, his tone lighter now.

Giselle laughed, the sound filling the room with warmth. "How about we start with something simple? Like making dinner without any international incidents?"

Tom grinned, feeling lighter than he had in years. "Deal. Though I can't promise I won't try to sneak some exotic spices into the mix."

As darkness settled outside, they remained by the window, content in each other's company and grateful for the love that had carried them through it all.

Chapter 20

Tom Beauchamp sank into his well-worn leather armchair, the springs creaking in familiar protest. The living room was a cozy chaos of dreams and possibilities, with stacks of travel guides teetering precariously on every available surface. The warm glow of the table lamp cast long shadows across the room, highlighting the vivid images of far-off destinations that adorned the covers of countless brochures.

Giselle perched on the arm of Tom's chair, her fiery red hair cascading over her shoulder as she leaned in to show him a glossy page. "Look at this, Tom," she said, her voice tinged with excitement and her slight Quebecois accent more pronounced than usual. "The Eiffel Tower at sunset. Can you imagine?"

Tom squinted at the image, his tired eyes struggling to focus after hours of poring over their options. He couldn't help but smile at Giselle's enthusiasm. Her green eyes sparkled with a fervor that reminded him of why he'd fallen for her in the first place.

"Paris, huh?" he mused, running a hand through his graying hair. "That's quite the dream, sweetheart."

Giselle nodded eagerly, her slender fingers tracing the outline of the iconic tower on the page. "It's always been my dream destination. The art, the culture, the food..." She trailed off, lost in thought.

Tom chuckled, a wry smile playing at the corners of his mouth. "Well, I suppose I'll need to print some more money first." He winked at Giselle, his tone light but carrying an undercurrent of weariness.

Giselle playfully swatted his shoulder. "Tom! Don't even joke about that," she admonished, but her eyes danced with amusement.

As Tom gazed at Giselle, he felt a familiar twinge of guilt. She deserved the world, and here he was, making jokes about their dubious past. He cleared his throat, pushing the thought aside. "You know what? Let's do it. Paris it is."

Giselle's face lit up, and she threw her arms around Tom's neck. "Really? Oh, Tom, thank you!" She planted a quick kiss on his cheek before jumping up and rushing to grab more brochures.

Tom watched her go, his heart swelling with affection. Maybe this was their chance for a fresh start, he thought. A legitimate adventure, for once. As Giselle returned, arms laden with more travel guides, Tom couldn't help but feel a spark of excitement ignite within him. Perhaps their best days were still ahead.

Tom leaned back in his armchair, a nostalgic smile playing on his lips. "You know, Giselle, when I think about our little... adventure, I can't help but laugh at how absurd it all was."

Giselle giggled, her eyes sparkling with mischief. "Oh, don't remind me! Remember when you almost got caught because you left that practice sheet in the copier?"

Tom's face reddened, but he chuckled. "How could I forget? I swear, my heart nearly stopped when I realized. And then there was that time we had to stuff all those bills into your oversized purse at the mall."

"I felt like the world's most ridiculous shoplifter!" Giselle exclaimed, doubling over with laughter.

As their laughter subsided, Tom felt a warmth spreading through his chest. Despite the risks and close calls, these shared memories had brought them closer together.

Suddenly, Tom's phone buzzed on the coffee table. He glanced at the screen, his brow furrowing. "It's Rosalie," he murmured, surprised.

"Your old lawyer?" Giselle asked, curiosity piqued.

Tom nodded, answering the call. "Rosalie, what a surprise."

"Tom," Rosalie's crisp voice came through the speaker. "I hope I'm not interrupting anything important."

"Not at all," Tom replied, his mind racing. Why would she be calling now?

"I've heard whispers about your recent... escapades," Rosalie said, her tone careful but intrigued. "I wanted to touch base and offer my services, should you need any legal assistance in your future endeavors."

Tom's eyebrows shot up. He caught Giselle's questioning look and mouthed 'later' to her. "I appreciate the offer, Rosalie. But I assure you, our days of needing that kind of help are behind us."

"Of course," Rosalie replied smoothly. "But should you ever need counsel for more... legitimate pursuits, my door is always open."

As Tom ended the call, he couldn't shake the feeling that Rosalie knew more than she was letting on. He turned to Giselle, ready to fill her in on the unexpected conversation.

As Tom set his phone down, Giselle's eyes sparkled with mischief. She leaned forward, her red hair cascading over her shoulders, and said, "You know, chéri, maybe Rosalie's onto something. Why don't we start a legitimate business together?"

Tom chuckled, running a hand through his graying hair. "A legitimate business? Us?"

"Pourquoi pas?" Giselle grinned, her accent thickening with excitement. "We've got skills, non? Just... not the kind you put on a regular résumé."

Tom leaned back, considering. The idea was tempting, a chance to use their talents without looking over their shoulders. "What did you have in mind?"

Giselle jumped up, pacing the room with animated gestures. "Oh, the possibilities! We could start a security consulting firm. 'We know how criminals think because... well, you know,'" she winked.

Tom burst out laughing. "I can see the tagline now: 'Let the foxes guard your henhouse!'"

"Or," Giselle continued, her green eyes twinkling, "a travel agency specializing in 'discreet getaways.' We certainly know all about those!"

Tom shook his head, amused. "I'm not sure that's the fresh start we're looking for, mon cœur."

"Okay, okay," Giselle giggled, flopping back onto the couch. "How about... a counterfeiting museum? We could display all the tricks of the trade. It's educational!"

"And probably illegal," Tom replied, but he couldn't help grinning. Her enthusiasm was infectious, reminding him why he'd fallen for her in the first place.

As they continued brainstorming, each idea more outlandish than the last, Tom felt a surge of excitement. Whatever they chose, he realized, they'd face it together – and that made all the difference.

Tom's eyes lit up suddenly, a spark of inspiration gleaming in their weary depths. "Wait a minute, Giselle. What if we combined all of these ideas into one?" He leaned forward, his voice gaining momentum. "An escape room!"

Giselle cocked her head, intrigued. "Go on, chéri. I'm listening."

"Think about it," Tom explained, gesturing enthusiastically. "We can create immersive experiences, design intricate puzzles, and tell stories - all while using our... unique skill set." He chuckled softly. "Plus, it's perfectly legal."

Giselle's face broke into a wide grin. "Tom, that's brilliant! We could have different themes - maybe even one about counterfeiters trying to escape the authorities." She winked playfully.

"Exactly!" Tom exclaimed, his measured tone giving way to excitement. "We could call it 'The Great Escape Artists' or something catchy like that."

As they sat side by side on the couch, Tom couldn't help but marvel at how quickly they'd transitioned from wild schemes to a legitimate business plan. He felt a warmth spreading through his chest, a mixture of hope and anticipation he hadn't experienced in years.

"So, where do we start?" Giselle asked, her green eyes sparkling with curiosity.

Tom reached for a nearby notebook, his methodical nature kicking in. "First things first, we need to brainstorm themes and puzzle ideas.

Then we'll scout locations." He paused, looking at Giselle with a soft smile. "Ready to dive in?"

Giselle leaned in, kissing him gently. "Always, mon amour. Let's make this our greatest adventure yet."

Tom squinted up at the dilapidated building, its faded brick façade crumbling in places. Beside him, Giselle wrinkled her nose at the musty smell wafting from the open doorway.

"It's... charming," she offered, her voice tinged with skepticism.

Tom chuckled, running a hand through his graying hair. "I know it doesn't look like much now, but just imagine the possibilities, Giselle. We could transform this place into something spectacular."

As they stepped inside, their footsteps echoed in the cavernous space. Dust motes danced in the sunlight streaming through grimy windows. Tom's mind raced with ideas, his eyes darting from corner to corner.

"Over here," he said, pointing to a far wall, "we could build a secret passage. And there, a hidden room behind a bookcase."

Giselle's initial hesitation melted away as she caught Tom's infectious enthusiasm. "Ooh, and what about a laser maze in that corner?" she suggested, her green eyes twinkling.

Tom grinned, pulling her close. "That's my girl. Always thinking outside the box."

As they explored further, Tom's phone buzzed. It was Jacques, their former employee from the counterfeit days.

"Hey, boss," Jacques's voice crackled through the speaker. "Heard you're starting a new venture. Need an extra pair of hands?"

Tom exchanged a glance with Giselle, who nodded encouragingly. "Actually, Jacques, we could use all the help we can get. How do you feel about power tools and paint rollers?"

Over the next few days, the old building buzzed with activity. Tom, Giselle, and their motley crew of former associates worked tirelessly, transforming the space into a labyrinth of mysteries and challenges.

As Tom carefully painted intricate designs on a newly constructed wall, he couldn't help but reflect on the irony of their situation. Here they were, the same group that once meticulously crafted counterfeit bills, now pouring their skills into creating an entirely different kind of illusion.

"You know," he mused aloud to Giselle, who was nearby assembling a complex lock mechanism, "I never thought I'd say this, but I think I prefer building escape rooms to printing fake money."

Giselle laughed, her red hair catching the light as she turned to face him. "Who would have thought, eh? From master criminals to puzzle masters. Life's funny that way."

As the day wore on, Tom stood back, admiring their progress. The once-derelict building was slowly coming to life, filled with secret passages, hidden clues, and mind-bending puzzles. For the first time in a long while, he felt a sense of genuine accomplishment, untainted by the guilt that had plagued their previous endeavors.

"We're really doing this, aren't we?" he said softly to Giselle as they took a break, sharing a bottle of water.

She squeezed his hand, her eyes shining with pride and affection. "We are, mon amour. And it's going to be magnifique."

The morning sun cast a golden glow on the freshly painted façade of "Enigma Escapes" as Tom and Giselle stood side by side, their nerves palpable. Tom's fingers drummed an anxious rhythm on his thigh, his eyes darting between the empty street and the locked entrance.

"What if no one shows up?" he murmured, his voice tight with worry.

Giselle slipped her hand into his, giving it a reassuring squeeze. "They'll come, mon chéri. We've planned this down to the last detail, just like always."

Tom smiled wryly. "Let's hope this turns out better than our last meticulous plan."

As if on cue, a group of excited chatter drifted towards them. Tom's breath caught in his throat as he spotted a small crowd rounding the corner, their eyes lighting up at the sight of the escape room.

"This is it," he whispered, straightening his posture and plastering on his most welcoming smile.

Giselle nodded, her green eyes sparkling with anticipation. "Show time."

With a deep breath, Tom strode forward and unlocked the doors, swinging them open wide. "Welcome to Enigma Escapes!" he announced, his voice carrying a warmth that surprised even him. "Who's ready for an adventure?"

The crowd surged forward, their excitement infectious. As Tom began ushering people inside, he caught Giselle's eye and couldn't help but grin. For once, the thrill they were providing was completely legal, and somehow, that made it all the more exhilarating.

Tom's heart swelled with pride as he watched through the observation monitors. A group of college students huddled around a cryptic map, their heads bent together in concentration. In another room, a family of four cheered as the youngest, a girl no older than ten, deciphered a complex riddle that had stumped her parents.

"Look at them go," Giselle whispered, her eyes glued to the screens. "They're loving it, Tom."

He nodded, a lump forming in his throat. "We did this, Giselle. We created something real, something good."

As the day progressed, laughter and triumphant shouts echoed through the building. Tom found himself drawn into the excitement, offering subtle hints when groups got stuck and congratulating them as they emerged victorious.

"That was incredible!" a middle-aged woman exclaimed as she exited the final room. "The attention to detail, the clever puzzles... I've never experienced anything like it!"

Tom beamed, his chest puffing with pride. "Thank you so much. We're thrilled you enjoyed it."

As the last group left, Tom and Giselle stood in the empty lobby, the silence a stark contrast to the day's excitement.

"We did it," Giselle said softly, leaning her head on Tom's shoulder.

He wrapped an arm around her, his mind drifting to their tumultuous past. "You know, for years I thought success meant having more – more money, more stuff. But this..." He gestured around the room. "This feels different. Better."

Giselle nodded, her red hair catching the fading sunlight. "It's because we're not just taking anymore, Tom. We're giving people something to remember, something to smile about."

Tom chuckled, a warmth spreading through his chest. "Who would've thought, huh? Two ex-counterfeiters finding honest success in make-believe puzzles."

"Life's funny that way," Giselle mused, her green eyes twinkling. "Sometimes the most unexpected paths lead us exactly where we need to be."

As they stood there, basking in the afterglow of their successful launch, Tom realized that for the first time in years, he felt truly content. The thrill of their new venture wasn't about outsmarting the system or accumulating wealth. It was about creating joy, fostering connections, and finally doing something they could be genuinely proud of.

"Come on," he said, giving Giselle a gentle squeeze. "Let's go home and celebrate. We've earned it."

Hand in hand, they walked out into the cool evening air, leaving behind the elaborate puzzles and secret passages. As they strolled down the street, Tom couldn't help but feel that they had finally solved the most important puzzle of all – finding their place in the world, together.

As Tom and Giselle approached their cozy apartment, the streetlights flickered to life, casting a warm glow on the cobblestone sidewalk. Tom fumbled for his keys, his fingers still slightly stiff from a day of last-minute escape room adjustments.

"I can't wait to kick off these shoes and open that bottle of champagne we've been saving," Giselle said, her voice tinged with excitement and fatigue.

Tom grinned, pushing open the door. "I couldn't agree more. Today was—"

The shrill ring of his cell phone cut through the air, startling them both. Tom fished it out of his pocket, frowning at the unfamiliar number on the screen.

"Who could that be at this hour?" Giselle whispered, her brow furrowed.

Tom shrugged, his thumb hovering over the answer button. A nagging feeling in his gut made him hesitate. "I'm not sure, but... something feels off."

He answered, his voice cautious. "Hello?"

A familiar, refined voice purred through the speaker. "Ah, Tom. It's been far too long."

Tom's blood ran cold. He'd know that voice anywhere. "Patrice?" he breathed, shooting a worried glance at Giselle.

"The very same," Patrice replied, a hint of amusement in his tone. "I hear congratulations are in order. Your new... venture... sounds quite intriguing."

Tom's mind raced. How did Patrice know about the escape room? And more importantly, why was he calling now, after all this time?

"What do you want, Patrice?" Tom asked, trying to keep his voice steady.

A low chuckle came through the line. "Oh, Tom. Always so direct. Let's just say I have a proposition for you. One that could make your little escape room look like child's play."

Tom's heart pounded in his chest. He thought they were done with all of this, but Patrice's words hinted at something bigger, more dangerous... and undeniably tempting.

"I'm not interested," Tom said firmly, even as a part of him stirred with curiosity.

"Are you quite sure about that?" Patrice's voice dropped lower. "I think you'll find this opportunity... impossible to refuse."

As the call ended, Tom stood frozen, the phone still pressed to his ear. Giselle touched his arm gently, her eyes wide with concern.

"Tom? What is it? What did he say?"

Tom swallowed hard, his mind reeling. "I think... I think our past might not be as behind us as we thought."

Also by Shane Reed

Most of my books are listed on SmashWords here: https://www.smashwords.com/profile/view/Shane_Reed

The Sniffing Dog Scam[1]

Suzie and her dog, Charlie, once lauded for solving cold cases, fall from grace as their deceit is revealed. Officer Tom James uncovers Suzie's scheme of planting human remains to gain fame. This true crime story explores the dark lengths one woman will go for recognition, leaving devastation in her wake.

Stale Mate[2]

In a bustling city, a beloved bakery faces destruction by a ruthless gang demanding high fees. The bakery owner, fearing the consequences of involving the authorities, is desperate. Nate, an ex-military hacker, and Amy, a determined journalist, join forces to confront the villains and protect the innocent.

Fool's Mate[3]

Debbie, a victim of romance fraud, seeks Nate and Amy's help to recover her lost money from Ryan, the scammer. As they track down Ryan, tensions rise, and a daring plan unfolds, leading to a high-stakes showdown. With emotional turmoil as the backdrop, the team navigates danger to ensure justice is served.

The Conning Couple Books 1-5[4]

Join the dynamic duo, a modern-day A-Team couple, in "The Conning Couple" series as they right wrongs for their clients. In each thrilling installment, they outwit criminals, retrieve stolen funds, and return them to their rightful owners. With their cunning cons and daring escapades,

---

1. https://www.smashwords.com/books/view/1609103

2. https://www.smashwords.com/books/view/1578203

3. https://www.smashwords.com/books/view/1541200

4. https://www.smashwords.com/books/view/1541183

The Sicilian Defense[5]

Nate and Amy, an ex-military hacker and an investigative journalist, team up to fight injustice in their community. When Italian cafe owner Caterina is swindled by a criminal scheme, Nate and Amy concoct a plan to return Caterina's money. With a mix of cyber savvy and strategic deception, they outwit the criminal and help Caterina while setting the stage for justice to be served.

The Queen's Gambit[6]

Nate and Amy, armed with unique skills, infiltrate a theater group, unaware of a sinister plot. As they uncover the truth, they balance personal lives and a mission for justice. In this heart-pounding thriller, they race against time, facing unexpected twists, to protect the innocent and expose the truth.

The Great Escape[7]

In a world where justice is elusive, Nate and Amy emerge as an unstoppable force against the dark forces of human trafficking. Nate, an ex-military white-hat hacker, and Amy, a fearless investigative journalist, join forces to form a modern-day A-Team.

---

5. https://www.smashwords.com/books/view/1530876

6. https://www.smashwords.com/books/view/1524256

7. https://www.smashwords.com/books/view/1510950

Don't miss out!

Visit the website below and you can sign up to receive emails whenever Shane Reed publishes a new book. There's no charge and no obligation.

https://books2read.com/r/B-A-LSDAB-CLOAF

BOOKS 2 READ

Connecting independent readers to independent writers.

Did you love *Conterfeit Capitalist*? Then you should read *The Sniffing Dog Scam*[8] by Shane Reed!

Suzie is an unassuming woman with a dark secret. With her canine companion, they were once hailed as heroes in the world of law enforcement for their uncanny ability to solve cold cases, their legacy takes a sinister turn as the truth behind their success is revealed.

Suzie and Charlie were renowned for their ability to unearth human remains, aiding in solving cases that had long gone cold. Their fame reached unprecedented heights as they assisted in high-profile assignments worldwide, even earning a feature on the popular TV show "Unsolved Mysteries."

Beneath the veneer of success lay a web of deception.

---

8. https://books2read.com/u/ba5Jnq

9. https://books2read.com/u/ba5Jnq

When Officer Tom James grows suspicious of Suzie's methods, a shocking revelation comes to light.

Based on a true story, this is a riveting exploration of the lengths one woman will go for fame and recognition, leaving a trail of desecrated remains and shattered trust in her wake.

Also by Shane Reed

A Conning Couple Novel
Checkmate
The Great Escape
The Queen's Gambit
The Sicilian Defense
Fool's Mate
The Scottish Game
Stale Mate
The Conning Couple Books 1-5

True Crime
The Sniffing Dog Scam
Conterfeit Capitalist

Milton Keynes UK
Ingram Content Group UK Ltd.
UKHW041912041024
449101UK00001B/97